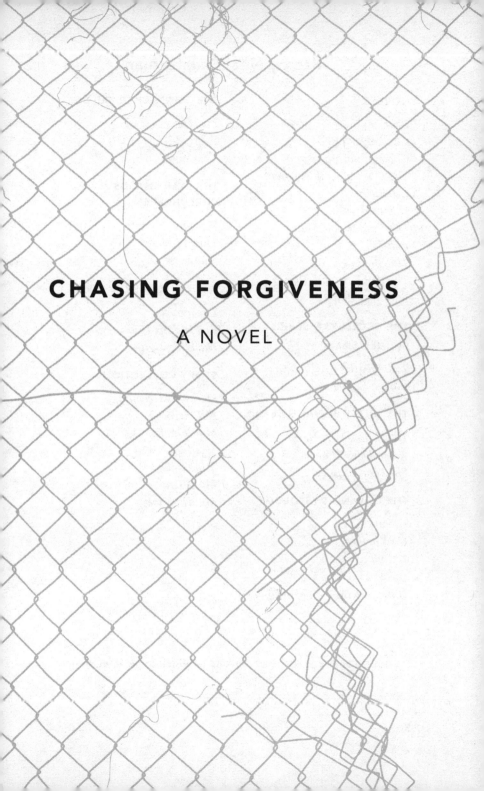

CHASING FORGIVENESS

A NOVEL

Also by Neal Shusterman

NOVELS

Bruiser
Challenger Deep
Chasing Forgiveness
The Dark Side of Nowhere
Dissidents
Downsiders
The Eyes of Kid Midas
Full Tilt
The Shadow Club
The Shadow Club Rising
Speeding Bullet

THE ACCELERATI SERIES

(with Eric Elfman)

Tesla's Attic
Edison's Alley

THE ANTSY BONANO SERIES

The Schwa Was Here
Antsy Does Time
Ship Out of Luck

THE UNWIND DYSTOLOGY

Unwind
UnWholly
UnSouled
UnDivided
UnStrung (an e-book original)

THE SKINJACKER TRILOGY

Everlost
Everwild
Everfound

THE STAR SHARDS
CHRONICLES

Scorpion Shards
Thief of Souls
Shattered Sky

THE DARK FUSION SERIES

Dreadlocks
Red Rider's Hood
Duckling Ugly

STORY COLLECTIONS

Darkness Creeping
Kid Heroes
MindQuakes
MindStorms
MindTwisters
MindBenders
MindBenders

Visit the author at storyman.com and facebook.com/nealshusterman

NEAL SHUSTERMAN

CHASING FORGIVENESS

A NOVEL

(Originally published as *What Daddy Did*)

SIMON & SCHUSTER BFYR

NEW YORK LONDON TORONTO SYDNEY NEW DELHI

This book is a work of fiction. It is inspired by real-life experiences that have been fictionalized for the purposes of this novel. Names and identifying details are also fictional.

SIMON & SCHUSTER BFYR

An imprint of Simon & Schuster Children's Publishing Division
1230 Avenue of the Americas, New York, New York 10020
Text copyright © 1991 by Neal Shusterman
Originally published in 1991 as *What Daddy Did* by Little, Brown and Company.
This SIMON & SCHUSTER BFYR edition 2015
Jacket photograph of sky copyright © 2015 by Thinkstock/iStock; photograph of chain-link fence copyright © 2015 by Getty Images/Jasper White
For information about special discounts for bulk purchases, please contact Simon & Schuster Special Sales at 1-866-506-1949 or business@simonandschuster.com.
The Simon & Schuster Speakers Bureau can bring authors to your live event. For more information or to book an event, contact the Simon & Schuster Speakers Bureau at 1-866-248-3049 or visit our website at www.simonspeakers.com.
Jacket design by Krista Vossen
Interior design by Hilary Zarycky
The text for this book is set in New Caledonia.
Manufactured in the United States of America
2 4 6 8 10 9 7 5 3 1
Library of Congress Cataloging-in-Publication Data
Shusterman, Neal.
Chasing Forgiveness / Neal Shusterman.
pages cm
Originally published as *What Daddy Did*: Boston: Little, Brown and Company, 1991.
Summary: A fourteen-year-old living with his grandparents learns his father is to be released from prison after killing his mother and feels apprehensive about renewing the relationship. Inspired by real events.
ISBN 978-1-4814-2992-4 (hardcover; alk. paper)
ISBN 978-1-4814-2993-1 (eBook)
[1. Fathers and sons—Fiction. 2. Death—Fiction. 3. Forgiveness—Fiction. 4. Grandparents—Fiction.] I. Title.
PZ7.S55987Wh 2015
[Fic]—dc23
2014016228

For "Megan"

PREFACE

I never thought it would happen to our family—not to us: I
mean, we're really civilized people. I thought those kinds of
things only happened to people that live in like . . . the Bronx.
  I don't have the faintest idea why Dad did it. Maybe
somebody knows why, but I don't.
  My dad didn't even *own* a gun . . .

                                                   —Preston Scott

I first met Preston Scott on a bright Sunday afternoon. He
was fourteen then, strong but slim, with a dark tan and tufts
of the blondest hair I'd ever seen. He didn't look like a boy
who had been through all he had, but the setting itself was a
constant reminder of the truth. He was living with his grandparents then, because his father was still in prison.

The home was in a nice suburban neighborhood. Out
front, kids rode bicycles down the street, and a neighbor was
washing his new sports car next door—as if nothing had gone
on at all.

Out back, Tyler, Preston's younger brother, did flips into
their pool, while Preston and I talked across the patio table.

Talking with him was not easy for me. I told him right
off the bat that I didn't know where to begin or how to talk

to him about it. Sure, I knew a little bit about what had happened to his family, but knowing did not make it easier to talk about. I felt sure breaking the ice would be quite a task.

"It's okay," Preston told me. "I can talk about it now, really." But still I smiled politely at him and stuttered as I spoke. I looked away from him. I simply couldn't talk about it to his face.

"Sometimes," Preston said, "when I tell people about it they start treating me differently—they become weird, you know."

Exactly, I thought—and what could I possibly say to him that wouldn't hurt his feelings? So we didn't talk about it at first. We talked about football and track—his two best sports. We talked about school and the weather, gradually getting to know each other, and gradually winding toward what I was really there to discuss.

Finally, the afternoon sun dipped low in the sky, casting shadows of tall eucalyptus trees across the pool, and a breeze began to cool down the patio. That's when I dared to ask him the question.

"Could you tell me about your father?" I asked. "Could you tell me what happened?"

And so he began his tale.

I listened, and as I did, I realized I almost didn't want to hear it—I didn't want to be this close to it. He told me the type of story you read in the papers or see occasionally on the TV news. It's easy to watch it on TV, because you can tell yourself it could never happen to the people you love—because they're all good people. Only bad people are capable of such evil deeds. You can judge the people on TV, and if you don't like what you see, you can change the channel.

But Preston couldn't change the channel.

"I go to sleep at night," Preston told me, "and I still pray to God that suddenly I'll be eleven all over again, and everything will be the way it was. . . . But God doesn't work that way, does he? The truth is that bad things happen to good people sometimes, and good people can do evil things."

I thought about that. Preston was right—but most people don't want to hear that. They want to be able to lock their windows and doors. They want to believe that all the evil forces in the world—all the demons—are on the outside trying to get in. But Preston showed me that those people were wrong. He showed me that the worst demons of all always get in long before we close the door, and they hide deep in some dark closet in our heads. Most of us can keep the demons in line and keep them locked in that closet by that part of us which is good . . . but if we're not careful, we may forget.

And we might lose control.

That's the evil force that kills millions of people . . . or just one.

On that day Preston, with tears in his eyes, told me what his father, Danny Scott, did, and through the next three years of his life, I saw the rest of the story unfold before my eyes. I saw a family journey deep into that black closet of their own demons—a closet that few people unfortunate enough to enter can ever escape from—and I watched them come out again.

Preston's is a story of life and death, of anger and forgiveness, of an unspeakable crime that no human being should have to endure, and the unbelievable family that not only endured it, but took the very bullet that shattered their world and used it to carefully rebuild their lives.

His tale is all of these things, but more than anything else, Preston Scott's story is a story of overwhelming love—the kind of love that can change the world—and if you never before believed in the power of love, Preston's story will make you a believer.

Neal Shusterman

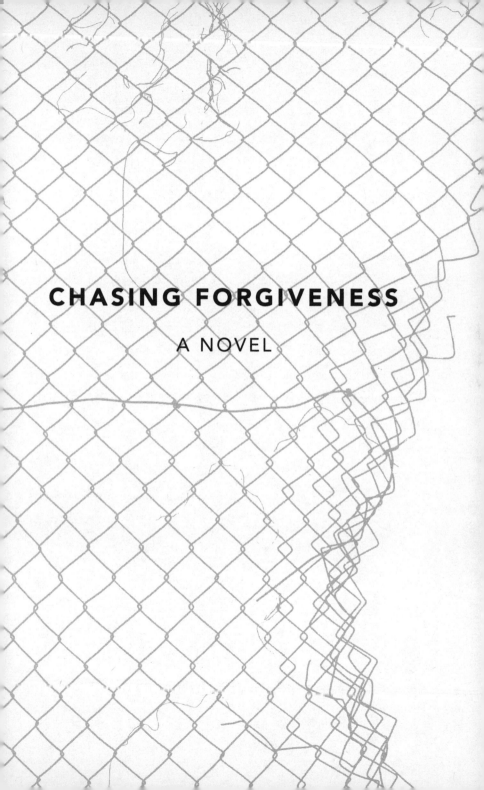

CHASING FORGIVENESS

A NOVEL

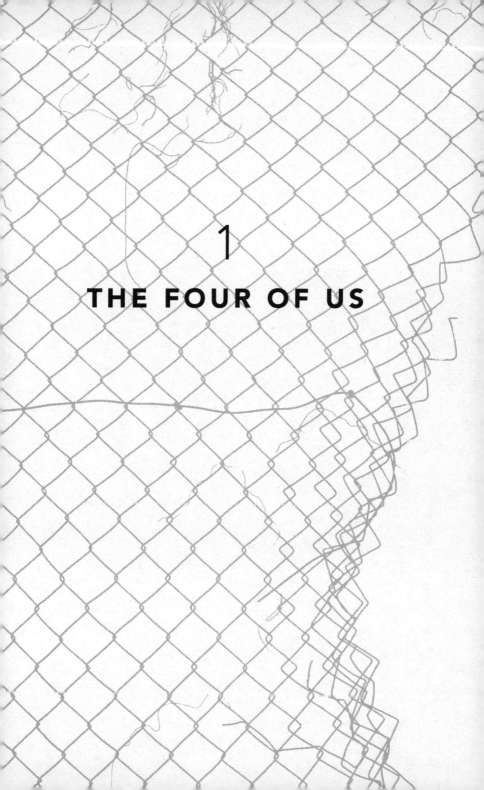

1

THE FOUR OF US

1

THE FEUD

April—Two Years Before

My hands are so cold, I can barely move my fingers. My knuckles crack each time I try. I see Mom under the bright lights, and my heart begins to claw its way up my throat. The butterflies in my stomach are turning into bats, and I think, What am I so nervous about? I'm not the one up there. But logic doesn't work when your mother is standing next to the game show host, in front of three television cameras and a packed studio audience. *Family Feud* is very serious business.

"All right, Megan," says the host to my mom. "Your sister got you one hundred and twenty points—you need eighty to win. Are you up for it?"

Mom smiles politely. "I guess," she says, and giggles a bit. I can tell she's just as nervous as I am. No, she must be more nervous. There are beads of sweat all over her forehead, replacing the ones they blotted off while she waited back-stage as Aunt Jackie took her turn giving answers.

Now it was all up to Mom.

Off to the side I can see Grandma Lorraine, Grandpa Wes, Uncle Steve, and Aunt Jackie, all waiting for Mom out of the camera's view. Why did they have to give Mom the anchor position? That's the roughest part—I know about that. If she messes up, she'll feel as if she lost the whole ten thousand. But then again, if she wins, she gets all the glory. I know about that, too.

The host begins his little speech from memory, like a policeman reading someone their rights. "All right, Megan, you'll have thirty seconds in which to give your answers," he says. "If you repeat any answers your sister gave, you'll hear the buzzer, which means try again. Are you ready?"

Mom nods. I can see her wringing her hands, out of the camera's view, as the host looks down at his question cards.

"A state," says the host, "that begins with 'A.'"

"Arkansas," she says.

"Children's favorite holiday."

"Christmas!"

Bzzzz! "Try again."

"Halloween!"

"A make of foreign car."

"Mercedes!"

"An animal you find at the zoo."

"Monkey!"

Bzzzz! "Try again."

"Horse."

She shakes her head immediately, knowing she goofed. That one'll cost us.

"A fruit you eat on cereal."

"Banana."

"A famous painter."

She doesn't answer. She's taking too long.

"Picasso!" she says.

Bzzzz! "Try again."

No answer. She's blanking out!

"Da Vinci," she says.

Dad, sitting next to me in the audience, shouts with joy. That must have been a good answer. The audience applauds, but it's not over yet.

"All right," says the host, "turn around, let's see how you did."

Dad stares straight ahead, concentrating on Mom. Like me, he feels like he's right up there with her under the lights. His hands must be cold, too, his stomach full of bats.

Without looking at me, Dad smiles wide and shakes his head in amazement. "She did it, Preston," he says to me. "I really think she did it!" He stares at Mom with a mixture of love and awe. Under the bright studio lights, she must look like a movie star to him. She does to me.

And all at once I know that Dad is right—that Mom has done it. Not just because Mom gave mostly good answers, and not just because we beat that other family in each and every round, but because we deserve to win. Because right now, everything is so right, so perfect, that it can't go wrong. It was simply meant to be—and when something's meant to be, no one on earth can stop it. Not even the host.

One minute later, we are ten thousand dollars richer. Dad is holding me and my brother, jumping up and down with both of us in his arms. We stumble out of the audience and down to the floor, and all of us hug and kiss Mom. Grandma, Grandpa, and the rest run out from the sides to join us. We all hold each other, jumping up and down in front of the cameras like imbeciles, but we don't care. This is our family, this is our day, and we can be imbeciles if we want!

Dad hugs Mom, giving her a big kiss, forgetting that my brother and I are between them. We get crunched and bounced around, but I have to laugh. The crowd cheers, and we get swallowed up in all the excitement and all the grown-ups around us. It feels like magic—like another world—and I silently wish that this moment would never end. That Dad would hold Mom like this forever, with my brother and me smushed tightly, tightly, between them—our whole family pressed so close together that my feet barely touch the ground. . . .

2

ONE MORE FEUD

January—Two Months Left

It's twilight now. Twilight should be a quiet time of day, but I can't remember the last time the sun set to silence in our home. Even in the backyard, I can hear them. Their voices cut paths through every room and out of every window.

In the dying light, my friend Russ Talbert and I do battle over a Ping-Pong table that stands in the thick grass because Dad hasn't been finding the time to mow the backyard. Russ holds his paddle Chinese style and awkwardly flicks his elbows up and down to give the ball some English. We both try to ignore the sounds of my parents fighting in the living room. Their match is much more vicious than our Ping-Pong game. Sure, maybe their fights are only words, but those words smash like fists and slice like knives. Maybe it's only words, but they might as well be tearing each other to pieces.

Russ and I play Ping-Pong and pretend not to hear it, but neither of us is any good at that kind of pretending. I wish I hadn't invited Russ over today. Maybe I won't invite anyone anymore.

"Do they always fight like that?" Russ finally asks.

"Not really," I say, although it's a lie. The truth is they've been fighting for months now. They fight about money, and about all the "things" we don't have. It's not like we're poor or anything; we've got a nice big house in a nice neighborhood, and we eat out and go on vacations to Hawaii and stuff—we can afford all that—but still, they argue. They argue about why we don't have a Mercedes like Aunt Jackie does, and why they can't make ends meet even though they're both working. It's always about money in one way or another. Nowadays, I hate money.

I liked money once, though. Two years ago, when we won on *Family Feud*, I thought money was the best thing in the world—especially free money. But free money doesn't last. Grandma bought herself a piano, and Mom and Dad put their share in the bank, and somewhere between then and now the free money disappeared. And now they fight. It's not a whole bunch of fights one after another—instead it seems like just one single fight that never ends, and I don't think any amount of free money could change it. Something's going wrong with them—something's going wrong with *us*—because my brother and I are part of it, too. I feel like we're

still smushed tightly between the two of them as they fight—
so tightly that I can't see where it's going to end. And sometimes I get scared.

"They don't fight much," I tell Russ. "Only once a month,
tops."

Russ looks at me with a half-smirk on his face, and it
really pisses me off. He knows I'm lying. He knows because
I'm the worst liar in the history of the world. It's like I've got
a lie detector wired into my spine that flashes above my head
to everyone "Preston is lying!" "Preston is lying!" There are
times I wish I could lie, though. There are times I wish I
could believe other people when they lie.

The Ping-Pong ball cuts across the net with a mean
backspin. I pull my arm back and smoothly smash the thing.
It skids on Russ's side, and his reflexes just can't match my
power smash. The ball flies past him before he even swings
his paddle.

"Just luck!" he says, and tosses me back the ball to serve.

Inside the house, my parents continue their battle, both
oblivious to the fact that I'm beating Russ ten to two. Or to
the fact that Russ is over here at all. Or to the fact that anyone
and everyone in the world can hear them. Their voices rise
and fall like ocean waves, and it's enough to make me seasick.

"They're really great people, most of the time," I tell
Russ, embarrassed.

"I know," says Russ. "Mine are, too."

I'm about to say, No, they're not—not like mine, but I catch myself and say nothing. Instead I just lob the Ping-Pong ball back to him slowly, giving him an easy shot for his third point.

No, my parents are very different from Russ's. First of all, Russ's parents are getting a divorce. They can't be all that great if they can't work out their problems without stupid lawyers.

Divorce really stinks. It's like going to the store and buying clothes, wearing them for years and years, then returning them and asking for your money back. That's what I believe. A store won't buy back a pair of used jeans, so how come people can trade each other in, like it was nothing? If your only pair of jeans is torn, you get a needle and some thread, and you sew them up, right? Parents should be the same way.

My parents aren't like Russ's. They're really big on family. "Family this" and "family that." To them, nothing else matters but the family, and so, whatever the problems are, we can all solve them together. And that's why my parents are great.

But I won't tell Russ that, or he'll start spouting at me all that junk he gets in family counseling. Well, the counseling didn't help much if they're splitting up, right?

Inside I hear my mom start to cry. I want to go to her, but I know I can't. Not just because Russ is here, but because when they fight like that they're on their own little planet, and I can't get through.

There are times when I've heard my dad cry. I'm glad he's not crying now, 'cause it would make me cry, too, and I can't cry in front of Russ.

The Ping-Pong rally goes back and forth until, not thinking, I hit the ball way in the air and it lands on the grass.

"Yes!" says Russ.

All of a sudden I begin to feel like I'm losing my breath, but I haven't been playing hard, so I'm not sure why. My face starts tingling, and I know it's turning red. There's this heavy feeling in my throat. Oh God, I think, am I going to cry after all? How uncool! Eleven-year-olds don't cry. It's a known fact. Not if they want to be taken seriously by friends and teammates. Of course my Grandma Lorraine always tells me that it's good for a boy to cry every now and again—but that's what grandmas are supposed to say. I doubt if she really believes it.

I stop the tears before they come, and I push them down, way down, into another universe entirely. I pretend nothing is wrong, but that lie detector above my head begins to blink again. Russ sees I almost lost it.

"Hey, listen," he says, thinking he understands completely, "fights are fights, and everyone's parents fight. It's no big deal."

"I know," I say, echoing his words. "It's no big deal." But deep down, I scream, Yes! Yes, it is a big deal! Because they never fought before—not until this year. They never fought, never had anything to argue about. They were perfect together—like that day when we won on *Family Feud*—and it wasn't just my imagination—I know because I was there.

"Maybe . . . ," says Russ, "maybe they should split up."

"No way," I say, real calmly. "Like you said, everyone's parents fight. No big deal."

The ball lobs back and forth between us without any power—like we've forgotten all about the match but didn't tell our hands or Ping-Pong paddles. The ball must be very bored.

"Lots of families are better off broken up," says Russ.

"Not mine."

"Lots of parents still stay friends afterwards—they just live in different places."

"Shut up," I tell him.

"It's great! You get to have two homes!"

"I said shut up!"

The brainless little Ping-Pong ball pongs on my side of the table, and before I know what I'm doing, I haul off and smash it with all the power my right arm can muster. It flies in a straight line—a white bullet, whistling through the air. In an instant it smacks Russ square between the eyes. I was aiming for his big fat mouth, but I still get my point across.

Russ throws down his paddle onto the table with a hearty bang and flies around the table to me, almost as quickly as the ball flew at him.

"Butthead!" he shouts, and he pushes me, and I push him

back, and he pushes me again, which, I've discovered, is the way friends fight.

Then I hear something, and I have to grab Russ's arms to end our little pushing war.

"Shut up!" I tell him.

"I was trying to help," he says.

"No, I mean shut up now!" He stops struggling, and I listen. "You hear something?"

"Of course I hear something," he says, referring to the world war going on inside the house. But beyond that I hear something else. I hear the muffled noise of a car engine, then a car door opening and closing.

Forgetting Russ for a moment, I race off down the alley on the side of the house, toward the front yard.

"What is it?" yells Russ, following close behind.

There, in our driveway, my little brother, Tyler, is being dropped off by one of his friends' parents. He fumbles with his papers and pencil case, with his lunch box and thermos. He has never figured out how to keep it all in his backpack. But then, he's only in kindergarten.

Tyler sees me coming out of the alley. "Hi, Preston," he says with a big smile. Tyler's a good kid. He doesn't talk much, but he always has this big smile on his face, and most of the time no one notices that he's quiet, because they're too busy trying to figure out what he's smiling about. That's what I like best about him. Everything could be going up in flames, and he would be smiling as if the whole world was a giant finger painting with a big blue house and a happy green tree and a grinning yellow sun.

Today, I don't smile back at him.

"Around back, Tyler," I tell him. "Don't go in the front way."

Tyler sighs, the smile slipping away from his face. "Again?" he asks.

I nod. From here we can see them in the living-room window, as if they are on display. Dad paces back and forth, shaking his head and gesturing with his hands. Although I can hear them, I don't listen.

I wave to the driver who is waiting to see Tyler get safely in the front door, and she waves back and leaves. I turn to see Russ, standing on the front lawn with his hands in his pockets. A little red mark shines on his forehead where the Ping-Pong ball hit him, but he isn't angry anymore.

"I forgot the score," he says, not too enthusiastically. "Who was winning?"

I glance once more at my pacing father in the living-room spotlight.

"You won," I say.

Russ nods. "I guess I'll see you tomorrow." He glances once at my parents, then jogs across the lawn and into the street. "Don't forget to bring your skateboard," he calls, and then vanishes around the tall hedge.

Alone with my brother, I lead him around to the back. As I open the back door, I help Smiling Tyler shove all his loose papers into his pack before they end up sprawled across the kitchen floor.

"What's for dinner?" Tyler asks.

"Who knows?" I answer. "Probably nothing."

We get to the hallway, close to the battleground, and I hurry him toward the bedrooms. We don't say anything to each other anymore about the fights. What's the use? Occasionally Tyler used to whisper to me, "I wish they'd stop," as if he were telling me a big secret. Eventually he stopped wishing it to me, when he realized I couldn't do anything about it. I always tell him to save it for his prayers.

I go into my room, and Tyler follows, since his room doesn't have a TV. I close the door, so now their voices seem farther away. Farther away, but still clear as a bell.

Tyler immediately turns on his cartoons—and laughs at Wile E. Coyote getting blasted by some Acme dynamite. But the cartoon explosions are never loud enough to drown out the voices in the living room.

Today it's Mom's turn to slam the door. And by the weight and direction of the noise, I know it's the front door. I can always tell how bad it is by which door slams. The bathroom door means they'll be talking again by the time the night is over. A bedroom door means somebody sleeps in the den.

The front door slamming means they may not speak for days.

In a moment I hear Mom's Cadillac start up and drive away. She'll go to Aunt Jackie's, I think, or Grandma and Grandpa Pearson's. Maybe she'll come back late tonight; maybe she won't come back till morning.

Tyler fell asleep without having dinner, lying on the floor, with cartoons dancing across the television. I turn off the TV and the lights and lie back, trying to fall asleep as well. Downstairs I can hear Dad busily working to keep his mind off Mom. I can smell frying meat, and it makes me hungry, but I don't feel like eating. I don't feel like leaving my room. Dad's always been a good cook, but over the past few months, it seems he's been having to cook for us a whole lot more. Not just cook, but also do a lot of other things that Mom used to do. It's like Mom suddenly got too busy at her job at the bank, or too upset, or just lost interest.

What I don't get is that Mom always says she would rather stay home and be a full-time mom than have to work. That's what she says, yet when she's home with us these days, it's almost like she doesn't want to be there either.

The door creaks open slightly, and a bar of light cuts across the dark room.

"Preston?" says my father. "You all right?"

"Shh," I tell him. "Tyler's sleeping."

"Dinner's ready," he whispers. "Cheeseburgers."

"Maybe later," I say.

Dad slips quietly into the room and closes the door behind him. I scoot over on my bed so he can sit down next to me.

"It's no fun having to hear us fight, is it?" he says.

I shift positions, leaning my head against his chest, as if to say it's all right. He begins to rub my hair and scratch my head like he did when I was really little and had a fever. It feels good. I squint my eyes like a cat being petted between the ears.

"What's the big problem?" I ask. "What does Mom want?"

Dad sighs, rubs his eyes, then says, "Don't blame her, Preston. This is my fault, not hers. I fly off the handle too quickly. I don't listen to her. I don't spend enough time with her."

Maybe he's right. Dad is kind of hard on Mom. He sets rules for her like he sets rules for Tyler and me. Dad's "old-fashioned" that way, and Mom must hate it—if I were her, I'd probably hate it. Maybe their fights aren't just about money after all.

But that's between them, and just because Mom has a reason to be upset with Dad doesn't mean that I do. Dad talks to me, he listens to me, and he spends lots of time with me. It's great, because I'm so much like him and we like to do the same things. We're always playing ball together, always fishing on weekends. Always racing each other. That's my favorite thing—racing my Dad. I'm the fastest runner in my age group, but Dad can always outrace me—only barely though. We race each other on the track, in the park, on the beach, any chance we got.

Although I'd never tell him this, or anyone else for that matter, I'd have to say my dad is kind of like my best friend.

It's too bad he's not Mom's anymore.

"Things are going to change, Preston," Dad says as he sits here on my bed. "*I'm* going to change. And then everything will be okay."

"I know it will," I tell him.

He smiles at me and brushes some hair out of my face. He gets up, then bends over, gently picking up Tyler. Tyler complains with a tiny groan, but his eyes stay closed and his body limp. Dad kisses Tyler on the forehead and carries him gently into his own room.

When I'm sure that Dad is back in the kitchen, I sneak out of my room and into his and Mom's.

Their bedroom is a big room, with lots of antique furniture. Some of it Grandma Lorraine and Grandpa Wes gave us; the rest of it Mom bought at all the antiques shops she loves to browse through. The carpet is thick blue, and on the walls are works of art and family portraits—just enough to fill the walls and keep the room feeling warm and homey.

I dive onto the bed, lying diagonally across it. The bed is so big and so soft, I could get lost in it. When I was little the bed seemed twice as big, and it was that much easier to get lost in—like when I would curl up in it on stormy nights or Sunday mornings. That was before Tyler was born. There was just the three of us, and we would talk and talk about anything and everything in the world—Mom, Dad, and me.

Of course, I don't do that sort of stuff anymore, now that I'm eleven.

But given the choice, I'd rather be five years old and lost in the giant safe bed than be eleven and in the line of fire between Mom and Dad.

So I close my eyes, trying to forget, and trying to remember. I feel the cotton of the bedspread billowing around me. Dim dark colors flow around the insides of my eyes. A spot of red where I had been looking at the light dims, then fades. For a moment I feel dizzy and the bed seems to be sailing around the room.

I start to dream before I actually fall asleep. I dream about school and about track practice, but mostly I dream about being five years old and disappearing in a place that's safe and warm.

3

ESCROW

February—One Month Left

Mom is off somewhere, and Dad is off somewhere else.

But Grandma Lorraine and Grandpa Wes make everything seem okay for an afternoon. Maybe it's because they believe everything *is* okay—and when they believe it, it makes me want to believe it, too.

I spend half the afternoon watching basketball with Grandpa in the den. Grandpa coaches the players on the screen as if he's coaching one of his high-school teams—but his wisdom is wasted on the Lakers, and the game is a lost cause by the end of the third quarter. Giving up on the game, I follow the soft sound of piano music into the living room.

Grandma sits at her *Family Feud* piano—a big white grand that fills up half the living room. She uses it to teach piano to neighborhood kids and to play sacred music. Today she sits alone at the keys, playing a hymn I recognize.

"That was your mother's favorite when she was a little girl," Grandma tells me, but I already know because she always tells me that.

On the wall above the piano is a portrait of Mom, Uncle Steve, and Aunt Jackie that was painted before I was born. They've all changed so much since then. Aunt Jackie was thin and pale, just coming through her kidney troubles. Uncle Steve was just a kid, without his thick mustache and all those muscles he got from being on the wrestling team in high school. Mom's face seemed free of any troubles. "Did Mom know Dad then?" I ask Grandma, pointing at the portrait.

"I'm sure she did," says Grandma. "She was sixteen when that portrait was painted."

I can't imagine my mom being sixteen—much less fourteen, which is how old she was when she met my dad. I know all about that—Grandma loves to talk about it because it's a beautiful fairy-tale romance, the type she could put in a little storybook on her knickknack shelf.

It goes something like this:

Once upon a time, there was a fair maiden named Megan Pearson, with huge brown eyes and long locks of golden hair. When she was fourteen she was swept off her feet by a dashing young prince named Danny Scott. They were each other's first and only true loves. They were married on Megan's eighteenth birthday and lived happily ever after.

Grandma was always wise enough to end the story and put the book on the shelf before the fighting began.

On the wall, Mom's smile seems to be the very center of the portrait. Aunt Jackie is beautiful, but Mom seems to be a step above beauty. Grandpa always says she's radiant in that portrait. Mom's smile is still radiant, but these days that same smile seems to be covering up the stuff going on inside her head. Dad says Mom's much too negative lately. "Why do you have to be so negative, Megan?" Dad says to Mom all the time. "With you, everything has to be perfect one hundred percent of the time, or it's no good at all."

Mom gets her perfectionism from Grandma, only with Grandma it's different. Grandma wants things to be perfect, sees them as if they already are, and feels wonderful about it. On the other hand, Mom wants things to be perfect, wonders why they're not, and feels lousy about it.

Dad calls it negative, but Grandma calls it moody.

"Both your mom and dad were always so moody!" she once told me. "When they first met they would sit holding hands for hours, being moody together." And then she had added, "They were made for each other."

Lately I've been feeling moody myself. I probably get that from both Mom and Dad.

Grandma looks at me as I sit on the couch, watching her play her music. She can tell that I'm feeling moody.

"You should learn to play the piano," she offers. "I could teach you." But I just shake my head. Music's not something I have in me. "Don't waste it on me, Grandma," I tell her. "Save it for Tyler."

Grandma just smiles and keeps on playing her sacred music, as if reliving that first time she was touched by God. She told me all about how that happened—how she moved to California as a little girl after her grandfather killed himself when the stock market crashed in 1929—how her father would beat her older brother and how she would escape by playing piano. She discovered music when she was ten. Her family was never religious, but one day she walked into a church where a woman was sitting all alone playing the piano. "It was the most beautiful sound I ever heard," she would tell me, and to this day Grandma swears that the Lord entered her heart on that day and never left.

When I look at her and talk to her, I know that it's true—there's something about her that glows. She's radiant, but in a different way from Mom. Sometimes I feel it so strongly, I think if I touch Grandma's fluffy blond hair, I'll get a shock.

I think about Grandpa, too, as I sit there trying to get lost in Grandma's music. Grandpa believes in God just as strongly as Grandma does—that's how they raised my mom, and that's how Mom and Dad raised us—but it all sort of gets washed out by the time it gets down to me. I don't feel half as godly as Grandma and Grandpa probably do. And now, as I sit here trying to get wrapped up in Grandma's music, I find myself getting bored. Music is not my salvation. I begin to wonder if God could possible touch me some other way. Through football maybe.

Actually, it's my parents he should touch, and make them stop fighting over idiotic things. Somebody ought to stop them, because I don't know what will happen if they keep it up.

Yes, I do know.

And I can just see Russ Talbert's mug smiling at me with that I-told-you-so sort of smile and him telling me what a good thing divorce is.

I swallow hard and ask Grandma a question that I kind of know the answer to, but I have to hear someone tell me. "Grandma," I ask, "what does *escrow* mean?"

Grandma doesn't miss a note. "It's a waiting period," she says. "Before you can buy or sell a house, you have to wait a month or two. That's called escrow."

That's what I figured. Nobody tells me anything, but I figured things out.

"So I guess Mom and Dad are selling our house, then."

Grandma hums her soft melody. This is no surprise to her. "Yes, they are, Preston." She has no problem with it, but I do.

"Where will we all live?" I ask.

Grandma takes her time in answering. She finishes her song first, and when the last note has faded away, she says, "Everything always works out, Preston."

Just hearing her say that makes me feel a little bit better. When I sit here with Grandma, I can see things the way she does. Everything needs to be perfect, but everything already is. Her home. Her family. All is right with the world. As right as a piano chord and the harmonies of a hymn.

"You don't *get* separated," Russ tells me as we hurl a football across a bleak, windy sky, "you just *are* separated. You *get* divorced. You don't have to have lawyers and stuff if you're separated. Separated is the easy way to be." I suppose he must be right, because Russ is the authority on such things.

I wish Russ didn't know about my parents' separation. But he can't help but know all about it, because when my dad moved out, he spent his first two nights over with Russ's parents, who are separated but are sort of still living in the same house. Now Dad's staying with Grandma Lorraine and Grandpa Wes. Russ thinks it's kind of funny that my dad ended up moving in with my *mom's* parents, but that's just how our family is. We're close.

I throw the football long—a perfect pass that falls right into Russ's fingers.

"Touchdown!" screams Russ. He imitates the roar of a stadium crowd and spikes the ball, doing a little dance that is a perfect copy of the way "Weavin'" Warren Sharp of the Raiders does it. Weavin' Warren Sharp made that little dance famous.

Seeing Russ do the dance makes me a little sick to my stomach, and I wonder whether he did it to be cruel or he just doesn't know.

Yes, he does know. He has to know, because he knows every stupid little thing about me. He stops his Warren Sharp dance and looks down, filled with guilt that might be real or might be for show.

"Sorry," he says. "Didn't mean to remind you."

"No problem," I say. "Warren Sharp's great." He tosses me the football halfheartedly, and I idly wonder if anyone in the world would blame me if I shoved the entire ball down his throat.

Instead, I just toss it back to him. "I'm going out long," I warn him as I turn to head out for a pass.

I like Warren Sharp. I really do. After all, he single-handedly brought the Raiders to the play-offs last year. He's got these huge hands that must have their own gravity or something because they seem to suck a spinning football right out of the sky—and once a football has touched the tips of his fingers it'll never touch the ground. Not until he makes it into the end zone and spikes it down.

I used to wonder what guys like him did when the season was over. I don't wonder anymore.

Russ lets the ball fly but makes excuses right away. "I can't throw that far—you know that," he complains even before the ball hits the grass ten feet short of me. I get the ball and bring it back to him for a second try. This time I don't go out as far.

My mom's been seeing Weavin' Warren Sharp for a few weeks now. I can't picture him and my mom together, no matter how hard I try in my head. It's not the fact that he's so large and compared to him Mom's so small, or the fact that he's famous and Mom's not. It's not even the fact that he's black and we're white. I don't know what it is, but I just can't hold both of them in my brain at the same time.

Mom first met Warren Sharp with Aunt Jackie when they went to Palm Springs—it was sometime after the house went into escrow and Dad moved out. At first I was just impressed to have his autograph and didn't think much more of it, but then he started calling, and Mom started seeing him. Mom says they're just friends, but Dad seems to think they're going together, and who should I believe?

Mom is always talking about how Weavin' Warren picks her up in his Ferrari and drives really fast on the freeway. I've never actually met him, but Mom says I will. I really want to meet him just as much as I really *don't* want to meet him.

Russ throws the ball, and it slips through my fingers, bouncing wildly on the grass. It makes me mad, because I never miss a good pass. I throw the ball back to him. "Try it again," I say. Russ mumbles about how perfect a pass it was, and I go out a third time.

It's this escrow business that's making me feel so lousy. It's not just our house but our whole lives that are in escrow. It's like we're all floating in this stupid place where everything is maybe here and maybe there. The only thing I can count on for sure is math quizzes on Friday, and that's not too thrilling.

Maybe when escrow's over and the house is sold, everything will be okay. Maybe I'll get used to the idea of me, Mom, and Tyler spending our days with Weavin' Warren Sharp.

But even as I think about it, I get chills running up and down my spine, and my skin shrinks away from the air around it, as if I've received the full potential of a severe gross-out. I don't know. Does this mean I'm prejudiced?

The spinning football cuts through the windy gray sky, out of my reach, but I dive for the thing. I won't miss this one—this pass is mine. I skin my elbows against the ground, but the ball lands in my arms, and I pull it close to me so it doesn't have a chance to escape.

"Touchdown!" yells Russ, but I will not spike the ball like Weavin' Warren Sharp. I will not do his little dance—not now, not ever. No matter how fast he drives me in his Ferrari.

It would be easy, I say to myself, to just hang around and wait until everything works out, like Grandma says it will. I could just go to school and play ball and go to track practice and come home and eat and watch TV and go to bed, letting everyone else make my decisions for me. They'll do that if I let them. Maybe that's okay for Tyler—he's only six—but it's not okay for me. I'll be making my own decision today.

Alone in my room, I close my shutters, jump onto my bed, and cry a little into the pillow when I think about how quickly everything seems to have fallen apart. I don't cry a lot, just enough to get some of the lousiness out of me. Kind of like letting a drop of air out of a bicycle tire so it doesn't blow up. I cry just a little—the air gets out, and the sadness turns itself into anger, which is fine. I like being angry a whole lot more than being sad.

Tyler comes in, turns on the television, and flicks the stations until he finds some old cartoon. Tyler is not sad or angry. He's just there.

I can't stand the way he sits there, so calm and quiet—so I turn off the TV, and Tyler turns it back on, and I turn it off again.

"Preston!" he whines.

"Keep it off, or get out," I tell him in a really mean tone of voice. The kind of tone that Mom hates for me to use on him.

Smiling Tyler doesn't smile at this.

Tears form in his eyes. Good. It's about time he cried about something that went on in this house.

He lies on the floor and sobs. I let him. I lie on my back looking up at the rough gritty texture of the ceiling. It's like looking at clouds. If you look long enough you can see shapes up there. Circles. Animals. You can find whatever you're looking for. I've seen lots of things. I've seen an elephant . . . a house . . . Jesus . . . Weavin' Warren's Ferrari. Only thing is, once you blink, it's gone, and you can never find the same thing again.

I begin to wonder if the house we move into after escrow will have the same rough-textured ceilings—or if they'll be flat and empty.

I get up and leave the room to tell Mom what I have decided to tell her.

In the kitchen, Mom has just gotten off the phone.

"That was Aunt Jackie," she says. "I think we'll all be moving in with her for a while, when we move out of here." And then she adds, "You, me, and Tyler," just in case I might have thought Dad was included in the package.

I watch Mom as she sets some water boiling. Even doing something as simple as boiling water, she is beautiful. Her long bouncy blond hair is the kind you see on shampoo commercials. The soft curves of her face and her smile could win the Miss America contest—and her face doesn't show a single sign of age, like some of my friends' moms.

There's something different about her now. It's something good, yet somehow it scares me. It's the way she moves as she cooks our spaghetti dinner—she cooks with confidence and control, as if she knows what she's doing and she's glad about it. Everything about her is like that nowadays. It's as if being away from Dad has given Mom her life back. It's as if she's happy. I don't know how she could be happy without Dad—I wouldn't be.

Mom turns to me and squints a little bit. She reads something on my face, but she doesn't read it right. "Don't you want to live with Aunt Jackie?" she asks. "It'll be great, just like it used to be—remember?"

"Yeah," I say, but I really don't remember much about when Aunt Jackie lived with us when I was little. I know she took care of me and that's why we're so close. It's like she was my second mom. But it'll be different now. She's been married and divorced since then. She has two kids of her own to take care of, and even though she has a nice house, I can't imagine the six of us all fitting into it.

Mom tosses the spaghetti sauce into the microwave and nukes it on low, so it'll be ready when the spaghetti is. Then she goes into the living room, clicks on the TV, and melts onto the couch, rolling the kink out of her neck and sighing. "It was a hard day at the bank," she says, but it's always a hard day at the bank.

Dad thinks it's her attitude and not the bank, but Mom has her own view of things. "I have no room to grow," she says when she talks to people about the bank and about her life at home. Room to grow. When she says that, I picture one of her big potted plants in a tiny ceramic pot. It gets lots of sun and water, but it's still dying because it's choking on its own roots. Mom's like that. But just because Mom needs to be transplanted doesn't mean that I do.

I stand off to the side of the TV and clear my throat.

"I want to go to Grandma and Grandpa's," I tell her.

"Dinner will be ready in five minutes," she says.

"After dinner, then."

She reads my face again, but once more she gets it wrong. "Don't come home too late," she tells me. "It's a school night."

"No," I say. "I mean I want to go there . . . to stay." I clear my throat again. I can't look her in the face. "I want to live with Dad."

There, I've said it. I figure she'll probably cry and it'll make me cry. She'll think I hate her.

"It's up to you, Preston," she says. "I know your dad wants you with him. If you want to move in with him, it's okay with me." And that's all she has to say about it. I try to read Mom's face, but the book is closed. I don't know what she's thinking or feeling. If she is angry or hurt she certainly isn't showing it.

I want to explain to her all the reasons. I want to tell her that I'm worried about Dad, because even though he's with Grandma and Grandpa, he's really all alone without us. Without me. Tyler's always been sort of a mother's boy, but Dad and I—well, we just *have* to be together now.

I think it would be a tragedy if we weren't together, and Dad's had enough tragedies in his lifetime. When he was a kid, his sister drowned right in front of his eyes while he was trying to save her. His father—Grandpa Scott—had a nervous breakdown because if it, and Dad has had to live with the memory all his life. He's always said that Mom and Tyler and me were the only good things to ever happen to him. If he loses us all it'll be like his sister drowning all over again. I have to be with him.

I want to tell Mom all this. I want to tell her that it doesn't mean I don't love her—I do—I love her more than anything . . . but the microwave beeps before I can say anything, like the bell at the end of the round.

Mom smiles warmly at me, as if to say it's all right, and gets up to check the spaghetti. "Call your brother in for dinner," she says. So I turn and do as I'm told. I don't have to explain it to her now. When things settle down, there'll be plenty of time for explaining.

Back in my room, Tyler still lies on his back on the floor, staring up at the pattern of the ceiling, his eyes darting back and forth like he's watching a movie. I don't tell him that I won't be living in the same house with him anymore. I don't even tell him that dinner's ready. I need a moment to think. Just a moment to be in the world away from Mom and away from Dad. I jump onto my bed and join Tyler in surveying the ceiling.

"What do you see?" he asks.

I squint and try to focus on the coarse grain of the ceiling. "Nothing," I tell him.

"I see a pony," he says. "And I see a big shaggy dog." He points up at them like he's pointing to stars. "You see?"

"No," I tell him. As I lie on my bed, the ceiling shows me nothing today.

4

THE MYSTERY HOUSE

Saturday, March 3—Five Days Left

"I'm not gonna tell you," says Dad, shifting into second gear.

"Aw, c'mon!" The car smells of new rubber from the wet-suit that he surprised me with today. I know it's just one of several surprises he has planned, and now I know that moving in with him was the right thing to do.

"Nope, I won't tell." Dad's got a smile on his face. He loves when he can string me along like this. I kind of love it, too, and I let him play, because it seems to be the most fun he's had in a long, long time.

"C'mon, Dad," I ask. "How close to the beach is it?"

"You're just gonna have to wait and see."

If he bought me a wetsuit, that must be a hint that it's pretty close to the beach. I can't stand the suspense.

We turn onto Pacific Coast Highway. It's pretty warm for

March; people in shorts walk along the sidewalk. Kids ride by on bicycles, steering with one hand and carrying boogie boards with the other. This is definitely a good day.

Dad's looking good, considering. Actually, he's not looking very good at all, but he's looking better than he did a few days ago. He's thin. His face looks like it's caving in on itself. He's thirty-one, but he looks like he's much older than that. And his eyes—that's been the scary thing these past few weeks. They just keep sinking into his head, getting darker. He's lost weight, too—twenty, maybe thirty, pounds. That's a lot for a man as thin as he is. He doesn't eat much at dinner, even though Grandma Lorraine is a great cook. He doesn't eat much at all. Lately I've been afraid he's gonna starve himself to death, but today I stop worrying. Today he had a Big Mac and fries, and he's smiling. This is definitely a very good sign.

He turns up a street that heads down toward the shore—one block, two blocks. Then the road dead-ends right at the sand ahead of us. Dad turns into a driveway. A two-story duplex house, three houses from the beach!

"Aw, no way!" I say. "I can't believe we did it. We bought a house by the ocean!"

"Not bought it," he tells me, "rented it."

He jiggles the keys in front of me. We go up to the front door, and I think, People live their whole lives hoping to one day get the chance to live in a place on the beach. And this house is ours.

Inside, the walls are bright with a fresh coat of white paint. The beige carpet is new. Although from the front the house looks kind of dinky, it's very long, and much larger than it seems.

The kitchen is huge. "I made sure to get a place with a nice big kitchen," says Dad. "For Mom."

"Look here." Dad strides to the middle of the empty living room. "Our couch can go here," he says, pointing to the wall beside the big brick fireplace. "And the TV there," he says, pointing to the corner. Then he walks over to the hardwood floor of the dining room. "We'll get a better dining set," he says, and then we walk down the hall toward the bedrooms.

I can picture it. I can see everything. I can smell chicken frying in the kitchen, I can hear the cartoons on TV, and I can see Tyler sitting in front of it and Mom complaining that he's sitting too close. I can even see myself coming home after school and collapsing on our couch, right here in this living room.

"This'll be your room," says Dad, swinging a bedroom door wide. "You'll still have your own room. And the one across the hall will be Tyler's. And this . . ."—he opens the door at the end of the hall into a huge bedroom—"this will be your mom's and my bedroom. . . . And—get this, Preston— your school is three blocks away—and *right on the beach!* What do you think of that?"

My head is spinning. It's all coming at me so fast, I almost forget the one small detail that sort of screws everything up.

"But . . . ," I say. "But you and Mom . . . you're separated."

Dad smiles, sure of himself. Very sure of himself. "Not anymore," he says—and those were the words I've been praying to hear for a month now. "I mean," he corrects, "once Mom sees this place, and sees that everything's okay again, everything *will* be okay again, right?"

I want to believe him. I want to believe that a big house and a nice car will make everything okay between them. But the way Mom talks it doesn't seem like getting back together with Dad is part of her immediate plans. From what I can see she's going on full-speed ahead without him, and as I look at this big beautiful home Dad rented, I think how weird it is that two people like my parents can be living in the same city and yet be on two completely different planets.

I wonder which planet I should be on. Mom's planet is flying out of orbit, heading off toward faraway stars, but Dad's is big and warm and has welcome-home banners plastered all over the place—and I'm tired of being in escrow.

"Do you like it?" Dad asks.

"It's great," I tell him, and give him this giant hug. "I can't wait till we move in. When can we move in?"

"As soon as your mom and I square things away," he tells me. "Maybe a week. Maybe two."

And it's as easy as that. I never knew how easy it was to believe someone, I mean really believe them. And that night, for the first time in a long time, I feel comfortable and relaxed when I get into bed. In my dreams I can hear the soft hiss of the ocean pounding against the shore far below my new bedroom. Just another week. I know it will happen, because Dad promised, and my father's not the kind of man to break his promises.

5

CHASING LIMOS

Sunday, March 4—Four Days Left

The moment we step up to the door of our old house, I know that something isn't right—but I don't say anything to Dad. Maybe if I don't say anything it will be okay.

Dad glances at me, then lifts his hand and knocks on the door. He has the keys—I know he has the keys; heck, it's still his house—but still he knocks, and it only makes me feel worse.

Neither Mom nor Tyler comes to the door, so Dad fumbles with his keys and opens it himself.

Inside it is cold. Cold and still. It's noon, and outside the day has turned sunny, but inside the curtains are drawn, and the nighttime chill has been trapped in. It even smells cold. I wonder how long it's been since the heater has been on. It couldn't be more than two days, but it feels like the place has been closed up all winter.

"That's odd," mumbles Dad. "The plants are gone."

Now I realize what gave me that creepy feeling when we first walked up. Mom's ferns—the ones that sat in big ceramic pots on either side of the front door—were not there. All that was left were brown dirt stains on the concrete.

And the plants in the house—our living room's always been like a jungle and our kitchen a rain forest, both filled with big leafy green things Mom had grown from tiny seedlings and cuttings—they were gone, too.

"Well," said Dad, "she probably took them to Aunt Jackie's."

But why take the plants? Was she afraid Dad and I wouldn't water them when we came?

Since Mom and Tyler are staying with Aunt Jackie, Dad thought it would be all right to move back in here until escrow was over and the new owners could move in.

It's been two weeks since I've seen either Mom or Tyler, and I was kind of hoping we'd bump into them as we moved back in . . . but who am I kidding? Mom has been out of here for days.

She wasn't going to risk bumping into Dad, I say to myself, but quickly shake the thought away. No, I correct my brain, she just wanted to make sure the place was ready for us.

But why the plants? Why not wait until the movers came and moved everything into our new house by the beach?

Dad and I walk slowly through the house, almost tiptoeing as if we were burglars, trying not to wake the sleeping people. In a way, it almost looks as if burglars have already been here. Some of the paintings have vanished off the walls. Some of the knickknacks have disappeared from the shelves—only Mom's favorites. And the house is so very, very cold.

Out back the pool is full of leaves and is turning cloudy green. Taking care of the pool was always one of my father's chores. I guess Mom didn't take it over when Dad left.

The door to Dad and Mom's room is ajar, and Dad slowly pushes it open.

I am not ready for what I see in there. Not so much what I see, but what I don't see—and in an instant, feelings I thought I had taken real good care of suddenly blow up out of nowhere, like an over-inflated tire. I can almost hear the explosion inside of me.

This is not my parents' room.

Not anymore.

Everything that could possibly remind me of Mom is gone, and the room is like a skeleton. Empty hangers line the closet like thin iron ribs.

The furniture is gone—the big antique chest of drawers, and all the delicate porcelain people that danced in frozen poses on top. The oak night tables. All that's left of the bed are four dents in the carpet where the brass posts used to be.

And there, piled on the floor, are all of Dad's things. They're not stacked, not folded, but thrown into a pile. Shirts and pants and shoes and socks and bottles of after-shave and books. It is as if some monster had eaten everything in the room, then coughed back up the things that belonged to Dad, and I think, *Why has Mom done this?* This isn't something someone just does accidentally or without thinking. She knew what she was doing—and she must have known how miserable it would make us feel when we saw it. She knew, but she did it anyway.

My mom used to be the best mom in the world.

How could someone so wonderful be so mean on purpose?

I want to ask her why. I want her to give me some good reason that I can believe, but she is not here, and I haven't seen her for two weeks.

It's as if she and Dad have spent so much time hurting each other over the past two years, they can't stop. It's like a sickness that goes back and forth between and is never going to end.

I'm crying now. Sobbing—really sobbing—and it makes me mad. I'm only glad that Russ and my other friends aren't around to see me act like a stupid baby.

Dad opens the door to Tyler's room. His clothes and toys are gone, and his bed is stripped down to the flowery fabric of the mattress.

And I think, What if they're not at Aunt Jackie's? What if they're nowhere? What if they just up and ran away to live in Brazil or some weird place where we're never going to find them? It makes me cry harder, and I can't catch my breath.

I hate her for doing this to Dad.

No!

I hate *him* for making me believe we would ever be together again. I hate him for lying to me.

No!

I don't hate either of them. It's this house I ought to hate or the people buying the house, or Tyler, or myself, but not Mom and Dad. Never Mom and Dad.

Dad comes over to hug me, but that's not what I need. I don't know what I need, so I push him away, and when I do, he starts crying, too.

"I believed you!" I scream at him through my stupid baby tears. "I believed we were all gonna be together again. You promised, Dad. You promised."

"We will be, Preston! Just give me some time. I won't break my promise, Preston. You watch! I won't."

His face turns beet red, like he's holding his breath. His face is so red, I figure blood is going to start coming out of his eyes instead of tears. And then, when I glance over at the mirror, I see the same shade of red in my face, too.

"I promise," says Dad again. "I'm not gonna let this happen to you," he says. "To us. To all of us."

But the truth is out, and he can't change that. It's been out for weeks now, but I just didn't want to see. He can't stop Mom any more than he can stop the day from turning into night.

"We're going out, and we're going to find them, Preston,"

he says real slowly. "And everything will be all right . . . believe me."

But now I can't believe him any more than I could believe in Santa Claus.

When Dad and I arrive at Aunt Jackie's, she tells us that Mom left early that morning.

"Come in and sit down, Danny," says Aunt Jackie. I can tell that the look on Dad's face troubles her. I can't help but think that this is all because of me. If I hadn't cried before . . . If I hadn't yelled at him . . .

"We were just having lunch," she says. "Please, Danny, let me fix you something to eat. You, too, Preston." She gently takes Dad's arm and tries to draw him farther into the house.

Dad shakes his head and won't move any farther than the foyer. "Is she with *him*?" he asks.

Aunt Jackie can't lie. She sighs. "Why should it matter, Danny? Why should it matter at all?" I can tell that Aunt Jackie is frustrated at having to be in the middle of this whole thing. She probably wishes that she could be anywhere else in the world right now, like I do.

"Was he here?" asks Dad. "Did he come in this house?"

"No," she says. Dad pushes and pushes, and finally gets Aunt Jackie to confess where Mom went.

"She's driving to L.A. She's meeting Warren at the convention center."

Dad starts to turn red again.

"Danny," says Jackie, "just leave it alone. Let it go!"

And I wonder what she means by "it." Let their marriage go? Is that what she means? How can she say that? I begin to wonder if Aunt Jackie's more on Mom's side than on Dad's. Why do there have to be sides at all? I don't want to be on anybody's side. If I'm with Dad, does it mean I have to be against Mom?

"Did she take Tyler with her?" asks Dad. Aunt Jackie doesn't answer, and that's answer enough for Dad. Of course she took Tyler. I try once more to picture the three of them together—Mom, Tyler, and Weavin' Warren Sharp—but I can't. My brain is far too small to imagine it.

Would Weavin' Warren give Tyler an autographed football? I wonder.

Would he let Tyler try on his helmet?

Would he hold Mom's hand in front of Tyler?

"Did you see what she did to our house, Jackie?" says Dad. "What she did to my things?"

Aunt Jackie looks away. "Just because she's my sister doesn't mean I know or understand everything she does, Danny." Aunt Jackie tries one more time to get us to come in and eat, but Dad won't oblige. He says a polite good-bye, stalks out, and I get sucked along in his wake.

I know Los Angeles now. I know the ins and outs of the streets and can read them like the lines on my palm. I've learned this in one afternoon, and when I close my eyes I can see the whole city sprawled out in front of me.

Dad is crazy this time.

"There are only so many limousines in this city," he says. "Especially in this part of town."

"How do you know they're in a limo?" I ask.

"Because I know," he says. "Either they're in a limo or a Ferrari. Stinking creeps like Warren Sharp always have limos and Ferraris."

But I figured it couldn't be the Ferrari. It's a two-seater; where would Tyler sit?

"Probably a limo," I tell Dad.

We've circled the convention center at least twenty times already, going down different streets, speeding back and forth through downtown Los Angles with the determination of people who actually know where they're going.

In front of the Museum of Science and Technology, we pass an old plane sitting right out in the middle of the pavement beneath another suspended high in the air from a pole. Maybe they took a plane. Does he have his own plane? If he does, that's probably why Mom likes him. A plane and a Ferrari and a limo.

There are more dented Chevies and wrecked Volkswagens around us than there are limos, but Dad doesn't notice all of that. He is a man with a mission, and I don't think he'll sleep until his mission is accomplished. I worry about him. I worry about him a lot.

"What do you think of Warren Sharp?" Dad asks out of nowhere.

"Me?" I ask, stalling.

"Yeah, what do *you* think of that creep?"

What do I think? Warren Sharp is what every American kid dreams of becoming. He's God's gift to football. He's fast; he's graceful. He's everybody's hero. He was Dad's hero until a few months ago. Now he's just a black man who screwed up his life. I've heard Dad curse him a few times under his breath lately. He never was prejudiced before.

What do I think of Warren Sharp? How would you feel if Superman flew down from planet Krypton and said to heck with Lois Lane because he discovers that the finest woman on this planet is your very own mom? What would you do if he suddenly flew away with her to the Fortress of Solitude, or wherever it is that Superman is supposed to live? Do you hate Superman for it?

What do I think of Warren Sharp?

"I hate him, Dad," I say. "I hate his guts."

"Good," says Dad.

The white limo we're following stops at a fancy restaurant and drops off a fat man with gray hair. Dad floors the accelerator around the sleek white car, nearly creaming the people next to us. He makes a U-turn and heads back toward the convention center. We'll never find them this way.

"That's the fifth limo, Dad," I say.

"Five less limos we'll have to follow," he answers.

Dad turns to me, then back to the road, and that one glance is enough to make my teeth start to chatter.

Used to be when Dad smiled, his blue eyes were inviting and friendly, but now they are hard and frosty. And there is something else in there, too.

I've seen a lot of scary movies. Things about people being possessed by the devil. Hollywood has all these neat special effects: pea-soup vomit, or heads spinning, or horns popping out of people's skulls and their tongues turning into snake tongues. They get better all the time.

But you know what? I think they've got it all wrong. If it really were to happen, it wouldn't happen like that, because the devil's much too smart. It would be small. Almost secret, almost impossible to see. If someone had the devil in him it would look exactly like the way my father looks now, as we drive around the Los Angeles Convention Center over and over and over again.

6

THURSDAY

I'm not sure exactly what day it happened, but I know it was a Thursday. I'll always remember it was a Thursday.

3:00

School was lousy today. I had an English test—the kind where you have to write a lot of long answers to short questions. I couldn't concentrate on it—my mind just wasn't on school. I probably didn't do too well.

I wait at my grandparents' house for Dad. He should be here any minute to pick me up so we can help time runners at Grandpa's track meet.

I like watching the high-school track meets. I get to be on the field with my dad while he times, and I don't have to sit in the stands. Someday I'll be down on the field, and I won't be just helping my dad time—someday I'll be running, and all those people up in the stands, they'll be cheering for me. But right now, I'm happy to be down there on the field with all the track stars.

Since all of Grandma's furniture is out being reupholstered today, I sit out on the floor of the living room to wait for Dad. He's supposed to be here at about three-thirty. I do some homework, and glance up at the front door every time a car pulls onto the street.

Wouldn't it be a trip if Mom came to visit just as Dad pulls up? Then they'd have to talk. They'd *have* to talk about Weavin' Warren Sharp, and about the house at the beach, and about why Mom is still living with Aunt Jackie.

I've been trying not to think about last Sunday, when Dad went on his wild goose chase around the convention center. I'm kind of glad we didn't find her that afternoon. Dad was being so weird about it, I wouldn't have wanted to see them. It would have been embarrassing to see Dad yelling at Mom in front of Warren Sharp and all those people at the convention center.

But then, Dad's not any better now than he was then. Maybe I don't want them to talk about it right now.

Maybe I oughta stop worrying. Maybe Grandma Lorraine is right.

Don't you worry about a thing, Preston, Grandma Lorraine told me. *These things always work out for the best. Your mom and dad are just going through a difficult time, and with God's help this will all work out and everyone will be much better for it. Everyone will have learned, because God doesn't give anyone a problem that they can't deal with.*

Sometimes, when I close my eyes and it's real quiet, I think about God and Grandma Lorraine. She seems to know a lot about that stuff, and I wonder whether she learned it or if it's something some people are just born with.

3:30

I'm bored with homework now, so I just lean against the wall in the empty room and rest. There are so many cars driving down the street that I give up trying to guess which one is going to be Dad. Instead I just try to figure out what kind of car is going by, by the sound of the engine. I don't look out the window to check if I'm right, so I guess I'll never know.

Across the large living room, Grandma begins giving a piano lesson to a girl with long hair, whom I recognize from school. I think she has a crush on me. Sometimes I think all the girls in school have crushes on me. Sometimes they come and wait in front of the house on their bicycles. My dad calls them the Prestonettes. It's really annoying.

Grandma's student plays slowly, and she keeps missing notes. Finally she begins to play something that sounds a lot less lame. I've gotten used to bad piano playing by now, on account of Grandma always gives lessons and usually the people who she gives lessons to are really lousy at it. I guess that's why they need lessons.

I wish Mom were here to play piano. Grandma plays really nice, but she always seems to play songs from church.

Mom plays songs that I know from the radio. Maybe not my favorite songs, but she plays them so nicely I like them anyway—and the way Mom sings! Her voice has won contests ever since she was a little girl. She could have been a singing star if she wanted to be, but she's not the kind of person who likes to be the center of attention, although she often is. When Dad fell in love with her way back when they were young, I think it was her voice that he fell in love with first. But I can't remember the last time Mom sang for Dad.

Don't you worry about your mom and dad, Grandpa Wes told me. *They've always been sort of . . . dramatic people. It's too bad you and Tyler have to be stuck in the middle—but just think about how good things are when things are good. Remember, Preston, the good times always outweigh the bad times two to one.*

4:00

Dad is never late. Never. That's one thing about him, he's on time to everything, and he never makes people wait. I figure maybe he forgot, and that's why he's half an hour late to pick me up—but Dad never forgets things either, especially something as important as a track meet. Maybe something happened, like he had a flat tire. I try to remember whether the spare in the back of our Rover was flat or not. If it was flat, then he would have had to get towed to the service station and get it repaired, and that would take at least a half hour, wouldn't it?

Then how come he hasn't called?

Well, he's embarrassed about it. After all, he always says he knows everything about cars, so he'd be embarrassed about going to a service station for something as simple as a flat tire. That's what happened.

Across the room, the musical scales go up and down, up and down, as the girl finishes her lesson with Grandma. A car pulls up into the driveway.

Finally! I get up to answer the door. Grandpa Wes will be pretty upset with us—they'd have been short one timer and probably had to start the meet without us. We'll have to hurry.

But it's not Dad.

The girl's mother is at the door, come to pick her up after her piano lesson. I let her in and look down the street, but Dad is nowhere to be seen. I could ride to Grandpa's school on my bike—maybe Dad went right there, thinking I was supposed to meet him there. . . . But he knew he was supposed to pick me up.

Maybe he was in a bad mood and just didn't want to have me along today. Would he do that to me? Probably not, but lately I don't know what he's going to do or how he's going to be.

I like your dad, Russ told me. *I think you did the right thing staying with him when your parents separated. You only really need to be with your mom until you're like eight or so. Then it's better to be with your dad, because dads are*

stricter and help you grow up better, you know? You're lucky.
I hope I get to live with my dad when my parents break up
for good.

4:30

I gave up sitting in the living room—at least in the den I can watch TV. I watch a recording of an old All-Star game. I like watching old games, because you don't have to worry about who's going to win. You can watch for the sheer pleasure of the game. It's like watching reruns of your favorite show.

Maybe Dad finally found Mom, and they're sitting talking things through, like they're supposed to. That would be important enough for Dad to just forget about the meet. If that were the case, I could forgive Dad for missing just about anything.

I never really understood Danny, I once overheard Uncle Steve say to Grandpa Wes. *But then, I never really understood Megan that well either. Who knows—maybe Danny's right. Maybe they were meant for each other, and it's just a matter of working out the kinks. Or maybe they're not. Maybe they just got married too young.*

5:00

Grandma bastes the roast she has cooking in the oven. We're having somebody over for dinner tonight, I think. Some homeless girl Grandma met through the church.

She peeks into the den. "Where's your dad?" she asks. "Weren't you supposed to help Grandpa at the meet?"

"I don't know where he is," I say. By now I've given up trying to figure out where he went. Maybe I had it all wrong. Maybe it wasn't Mom and Warren Sharp who were going to run away to Brazil after all. Maybe it was my father. Maybe he just took a plane and flew away. Would he do that?

Grandma thinks for a moment. "Well, the best laid plans . . . ," she says, which I believe is the beginning of a saying, but I've never heard it finished, so I don't know.

Mommy and Daddy really don't have to fight so much, Tyler once said. *They should just play Ping-Pong or Nintendo or something every time they feel like fighting, and whoever wins gets their way.*

6:00

The All-Star game is halfway over. Dinner is almost ready.

A car pulls up into the driveway, and I get up to greet my father. I figure I'll say something like, "Nice going, Dad," and sort of make him feel just a little bit bad for making me wait all afternoon and half the night for him to show up. Grandma Lorraine opens the front door. There are two men there: one dressed in a jacket and tie, one dressed in a policeman's uniform. They stand at the threshold and mumble something to my grandma. Outside the window I can see the police car.

"I'm afraid we have bad news for you."

I can't hear the rest.

But Grandma suddenly goes stiff as a board. She takes a deep breath and closes her eyes, then takes a second breath.

And suddenly it seems as if the air pressure in the house has dropped, as if someone has opened a window into space. The air has been sucked out, I can't seem to breathe, and the horrible silence around me is unbearable. It's as if time itself has just died of shock.

Grandma should be screaming; I know it's that bad. She should let off a wail so deep and so powerful that it shakes the house like a sonic boom . . .

. . . but I hear nothing. Grandma stands there silently and doesn't move. She floats in space.

And I know what's good for me.

I turn and I get out of there as fast as I can.

I go back into the den and I close the door. I lock it. I go to the screen door leading to the patio, and I lock that, too, and then I pull the curtains. I sit on the sofa, and I turn up the volume on the TV. Seventh inning. The crowd is loud in my ears.

No one comes to get me. I thought they would, but they don't. I have to peek out of the room every once in a while to see what's going on, because as much as I don't want to know, I have to know. I have to.

The first time I look out, Grandma is lying stretched out on the floor of the empty living room. At first I'm afraid that she's fainted, but then I see that she's awake and calm. Still in control.

The second time I look out, Grandpa is there. I see him for an instant. He is shaking. He is crying. I close the door before I can see any more.

The third time I look out, I can see Grandma, sitting on the piano bench facing the wrong way. She is talking on the phone. She is talking to Aunt Jackie. Something about my mother.

I slam the door again. This can't be about Mom. This can't be. I won't even try to guess what happened. A car accident. A plane crash. I won't even try to guess. I don't want to know what, and I don't want to know who, and I don't want to know where or when. I want to watch baseball. I want to sit here all by myself forever and watch this stupid baseball game and I never want to come out and I never want to know anything ever again ever. Ever.

Something terrible has happened. But if I stay here long enough, then maybe it won't be real. If I can make it go away for the rest of the night, maybe I can make it go away for tomorrow and the next day. Maybe I can make it go away for the rest of my life. Maybe I can push it so far down, I can make it not be true. Whatever it is.

The last side retires. The All-Star game is over. The crowd cheers. I watch it over again. I don't care that I've just seen it. I don't care.

Nobody bothers me.

Not for a long time. Then I hear the doorknob turn and wiggle. They can't get in—it's locked. Good.

They knock. I pretend I don't hear it.

"Preston?" It' s Grandma. "Preston, let me in," she says. Outside I can hear people coming into the house. People crying and moaning. I hear our pastor's voice out there. Oh, God. This must be really, really bad if the pastor had to come by.

I turn the lock on the door, and Grandma opens it, stepping in. "Preston, can I talk to you?" she asks.

I shrug and refuse to take my eyes off the TV.

Grandma sits down in a chair, with perfect piano posture. She gently grabs the remote control from my hand, finds the right button, and turns off the TV. I hate her for doing that. I hate her for coming in here and making me hear what she has to tell me. And I don't care if God hates me for feeling that way.

"Preston," says Grandma, as calmly as she would teach someone to play piano. She takes a long time—as if taking a long time could really make a whole lot of difference now. She takes both of my hands.

"You've heard what's going on in the living room," she says, so kindly, so gently, as if all her emotions and fears have been wrapped in a thick, warm quilt. But not mine. My feelings are cold and raw, and there is no blanket for me.

"You've heard what's going on," she says, "and I think you already know . . . your mother is dead."

I don't say anything at first. I try to breathe like she breathed when the police told her. Slowly and deeply.

"Now, Preston, there's lots of people who do fine without their mothers," she says.

"Like Abraham Lincoln," I mumble—a stupid fact that I learned today in school. I never thought I'd ever need to know it.

I try to keep it together, but I can't. I close my eyes and my brain goes into convulsions. I pray to God that she's lying or that she's wrong. Let it be anyone else, God, *anyone*. Let it be me instead—I don't care. Not my mom.

When I open my eyes, I can't see. They are filling with tears so quickly my whole head is flooded. My ears are clogged; my throat is clogged; I can't breathe. When I speak, I cough up the words, unable to say them all in one breath.

There's only one thing I want to know—the one thing in the world I know for sure I can still have—and nobody's going to stop me from having it.

"I want my father. I want to be with my dad!" I scream out.

Grandma looks away from me.

"You can't be with him, Preston."

"I want my dad!" I scream. "I want him now! Now! *I want my dad now!*"

"Preston," says Grandma. "You can't be with your dad . . . because it's your dad who killed your mom." She squeezes my hands tighter. "He shot her."

I rip my hands away and cover my ears, but it doesn't make a difference, because the words already made it into my brain, and the wail I let out breaks the silence of space and rocks the house like a sonic boom.

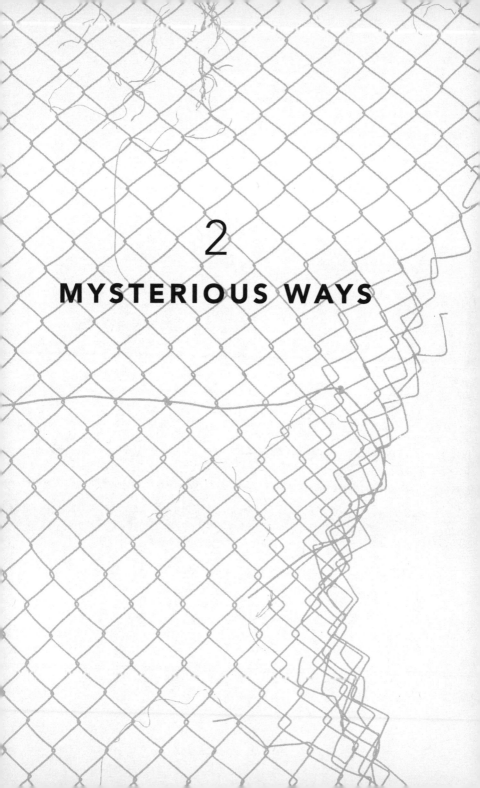

2

MYSTERIOUS WAYS

7

MY CLOSET DOOR

April—One Month After

The whole world seems to spin. Things around me change. I feel like I'm being sucked into a vacuum and I can't see where I'm going—but I know where I'll end up. The closet.

I forget where I just was, or what was going on, or what I was thinking about. The walls close in around me and move closer until I can feel the rough brush of jackets against my back, a wall to the right, a wall to the left, and the door in front of me. There is no light. There is no air. And something horrible is going on.

I know this is a dream. I've been here before, and it's always a dream, so I know that much, but knowing it's a dream doesn't make it any better. I'm locked in my closet, and there is no air, and something is coming to get me. A monster is going to get me. And I can't get out of the closet. I reach for the knob but can't find it. I'm so afraid, I can't breathe.

I touch the knob. It is hot—maybe there's a fire on the other side of the door.

Maybe it's not a monster; maybe it's a fire. Maybe the whole house is on fire, and I'm stuck here in this closet.

I grip the knob, but it's covered with grease. My fingers slip around it—I grip it until my knuckles ache, but my fingers still just slide off. Now the jackets behind me that hang from hangers far above my head seem to push closer. The jackets have hands. Hands slip out of the sleeves—thick, dark woolen gloved hands, but I can't see them, I can just feel them. They're going to get me—it's not a fire at all.

It's ghosts.

"Preston, I'm coming."

I can hear my mother's voice. She's far away now, in another room, but I know she's running closer, moving through the house, looking for me.

I try to scream to her that I'm here, trapped in this evil closet, but no sounds come out of my mouth. Only she can let me out; I know that. Dad can't let me out; Grandma and Grandpa can't. She's the only one whose fingers won't slip off the doorknob—I know that as sure as I know that I'm going to die in this closet if she doesn't get here soon.

"Preston, I'm coming," I hear her say again—only she sounds no closer than before, and I try to scream to her so she knows where I am, but still I make no noise.

The hands behind me—the sleeves of the heavy winter coats—begin to slide around my waist, and tighten. They're not ghosts at all.

They're snakes.

Big constricting snakes—that are going to squeeze the life out of me and swallow me whole.

"Preston, I'm coming."

But she's not. She's no closer. Maybe she's locked in a closet far away, too. Maybe her closet doesn't even have a doorknob.

I press against the door with all my might, and cry.

"Preston, I'm coming." She's even farther away now. I spin around and try to get the snakes off me. They slip off and turn back into sleeves.

But now I hear something. Someone. There's someone in the room here with me, standing just behind me. I can hear the breathing. And even in the darkness I think I can see. I know who this is. The blond hair, the blue eyes. It was never monsters or a fire, or ghosts or snakes at all. It's—

I leap up in bed so suddenly, so quickly, that all the muscles in my stomach tie into a knot, and I can't straighten myself out. My legs cramp, and I crumple into a ball. The sheets are soaking wet. I wonder if it's all sweat or if I was so scared that I wet the bed. Would I do that?

I look at my digital clock. It's only two in the morning. At least three more hours until even the tiniest bit of light will come into the room.

I can still hear Mom's voice, and I have to think about how much of it was a dream and how much of it was real.

Then the door opens and in walks Mom.

"Preston?"

I gag on my own saliva.

"Preston, are you all right?" She sits on my bed, and I hug her tightly, trying to believe that it's true. But the more tightly I hold on, the more quickly she slips away. In the dark, it does look like Mom, but I know that it is Aunt Jackie.

After the funeral, things were supposed to go back to normal. That's what Grandma said. But this is not normal. It's been more than two weeks, and there are no chores. There are no plans. I don't go to school anymore. I don't go out much anymore. I just eat, sleep, and sit in Aunt Jackie's living room, watching TV. And I have nightmares.

Aunt Jackie dries my tears as if I am a small child. "Do you want me to stay in here with you for a while?"

I shake my head no. "What time do we go to Grandma and Grandpa's tomorrow?" I ask her.

"About noon," she says. She seems a bit hurt that I'm in such a hurry to go, but living with Aunt Jackie is just too close to being with Mom. And besides, Aunt Jackie knows she can't handle having us here. Especially after what Tyler did yesterday.

She gives me a kiss. "Call if you need anything, Preston. Just call." She leaves the door open a crack as she goes.

And when she is gone, Tyler, lying awake on the bed on the other side of the room, asks the Question of the Week.

"When's Mommy coming back?" he mumbles.

"Go to sleep," I tell him. I never want to talk about this with Tyler. Let Grandma explain it. She's better at it. He knows she's dead—he was at the funeral—but he just doesn't get it.

"When's Daddy coming back?" he asks.

I pretend to be asleep, and eventually Tyler nods back off. Tyler may not understand, but I do. I understand perfectly.

My dad shot my mom and then shot himself.

I can say it, because it feels like it's not really happening to me. The words just don't mean anything anymore if I keep saying them over and over. Dad shot Mom, Dad shot Mom. I've said it to myself so much that I don't feel a thing. That's how come I can sit and watch TV all day. I don't think I ever want to do anything else.

Dad's in jail.

He's in the hospital of some jail somewhere, recovering from the gunshot wound he gave himself. He sits there, and I don't know what he does or what he thinks about. Maybe he just sits and watches TV all day, too.

I close my eyes and try to force myself back to sleep by thinking of football, but that backfires, because all I can see is Weavin' Warren Sharp.

I don't think we'll ever hear from him again—he managed to weave himself out of this situation with the same skill he brings to a football field. I wish I could blame the whole thing on him, but I can't because it wasn't his fault.

"Warren Sharp wasn't dating your mom," says Grandma. "She just met with him a couple of times—she was star-struck, that's all." You'd never know it was just a couple of times by the way Mom talked about it and by the way Dad reacted. I guess I'll never be sure of the truth, though, because I don't think any of us will ever mention Warren Sharp's name again.

Thinking of this does not help me fall asleep, so I change gears in my brain, and I think about the most comforting thing anyone has said to me. It was one of Grandma's friends on that awful Thursday night, when we all sat on the floor in the empty living room, reeling from the blow of what Dad had done.

"You'll see her someday," the woman said. "You'll see her again in heaven."

I know this is true. It must be true, because if it's not, how can I keep from going crazy?

So I will see my mom in heaven. But for now, I'm here in this room, so I pull the covers over my head and pretend that I'm already there. I wonder what Mom does all day in heaven. Does she float around? Does she play the harp? Do you look down on us, Mom? Do you see me there? Are you outside my room trying to turn the doorknob?

If you can't come to me, then I'll come to you. I'll die and go to heaven just as soon as I can.

• • •

The next morning, Aunt Jackie piles us and our suitcases into her newly damaged Mercedes and drives us to Grandma and Grandpa's, where I think we'll be living for a long, long time.

Tyler sits in the back playing with Legos, oblivious to the shreds of the convertible top flapping in the wind.

I sit on the passenger side and look at Aunt Jackie, thinking how, from this angle, she really does look like Mom.

She sees me and smiles slightly, knowing what I am thinking. "Your mom was prettier than I am."

"No," I tell her, "she's just pretty in a different way." I try to imagine Mom's face as it really is, but I can't. All I can see is the way it was at the funeral. All still. All frozen, there in the coffin. There were flowers all around, and I remember thinking how stupid it was to kill a bunch of flowers and stick them around a dead person. You'd think they'd at least let the flowers live.

Mom was wearing a pink dress. Someone did her hair and makeup. It wasn't the way she did it, and it made me mad. I wondered if she'd be stuck that way in heaven forever—in someone else's makeup, wearing someone else's hairstyle.

"The Lord works in mysterious ways."

This is what people tell you at funerals. It's because they can't think of something original to say, so they say the same old stuff because it's better than saying nothing. I wish they would just say nothing.

"What a terrible, terrible thing," they say, and then they cry for you. Why do they have to do that? Don't they know that you've cried enough already? You don't need people to help you cry. Death would be a lot better without funerals, or at least without the people who go to funerals.

I kissed Mom as she lay there, surrounded by all those dying flowers and crying friends. I half believed that, like Sleeping Beauty, her eyes would open when I kissed her cheek. I prayed to God she would just sit right up, and smile and say hello, but I knew it wouldn't happen; God's ways aren't *that* mysterious. Her cheek was cold when I kissed her—frozen—and I cried because I knew she wouldn't kiss me back.

Grandma and Grandpa sniffled a bit, and they spoke to her, telling her they loved her. They spoke quietly, like they were afraid to wake her. Grandma took it very well—all wrapped in that invisible quilt—filled with the Peace she said God brought to her the moment the policeman first came to the door. I don't have quite the same peace. Maybe God just hasn't gotten around to me yet.

Tyler just stood there and looked at her, like he'd look at a picture. It hadn't really hit him yet. It didn't hit him until yesterday.

Halfway to Grandma and Grandpa's house, we come over a hill, and the view before us is spectacular. The air is clear, and the sun peeks in and out of big billowing clouds that are swept across the sky by a strong wind.

"Aunt Jackie," asks Tyler, "do you think my mom is helping God hang clouds today?"

I think I'll always have two images of my brother fixed in my mind. The image of him asking wide-eyed, innocent six-year-old questions about Mom hanging clouds with God, and then the image of him yesterday taking that knife and slashing the convertible roof of Aunt Jackie's car over and over and over again.

"What do we do about Danny?" Grandpa says to Grandma, because he thinks I am asleep in my room. "What do we do?"

It's early Wednesday morning, just a few days after Tyler and I moved in with them. It's raining, and it's so dark out, I don't know whether the sun has risen yet. I stand in the hallway, just out of view, my back pressed firmly against the wall. Then I poke my head out, trying to stay in the shadows. Grandma and Grandpa sit in the breakfast nook, drinking coffee, dressed in bathrobes and slippers.

"What do we do about Danny?"

Grandma doesn't have an answer right away. This is the first time since the day of . . . since the day *it happened* that I've heard them talk about Dad. Well, sure, I mean they talk about him, but they don't really *talk* about him. Grandma gives me "weather reports" about Dad. "It's sunny today. Could rain later. Danny's healing nicely. Bit windy this morning." That's how they've talked for the past two weeks.

But the way Grandpa's talking now, it sounds big. Maybe

I'll hear something important—the type of thing they'll never talk about with me.

"What do we do about Danny?"

Grandpa sounds tired of life. He seems older than I've ever remembered him.

"This is a test, Wes," Grandma finally answers. "A test of our faith."

I wonder what she means. How do you pass a test of faith? What happens to you if you fail?

"You know what they're saying," says Grandpa. "They're saying it was premeditated. That he planned it. Good Lord, he borrowed the gun three weeks before it happened. What should we do?"

"He had a breakdown," says Grandma. "You know that. We all know that. You saw how strange he was acting. He lost thirty pounds. He never slept. . . ."

"Three weeks, Lorraine! Who knows what was going through his mind for three weeks."

"You *know* Danny!" says Grandma with more authority in her voice than I ever knew she had. "You've known him since he was fifteen! He's a good, good man. He's just sick . . . terribly sick."

Grandpa rubs his eyes and takes a gulp of coffee. "They'll throw the book at him," he says. "He could be in prison for the rest of his life."

Grandma doesn't say anything. She just sips her coffee, letting Grandpa sort it out for himself.

Grandpa takes a few moments to get his thoughts together.

"Everyone thinks we should testify against him—help put him away—and make sure he never gets near the boys ever again," he says. "They say that's the only way to put this behind us." He puts his cup down because his hand is shaking. The rain pats the patio awning. "It would be so much easier if I could just hate Danny," he says, "but I can't."

"Hating him won't bring Megan back," says Grandma.

Grandpa nods. "It won't do the boys any good either." He looks at the steam rising from his coffee.

"Can we forgive him?" Grandpa asks himself.

And Grandma answers, "I forgave him the moment I heard what he'd done."

They sit there for a long time, not saying anything. The sound of the rain hitting the patio awning fills the silence. Finally Grandpa reaches out and takes Grandma's hand, and he speaks to her in a soft, desperate whisper.

"Pray with me, Lorraine," he says.

And for a moment, it seems to me that the rain gets lighter.

I turn and head back toward my room, but before I do, I take a side trip into Tyler's room. In a few days of living with our grandparents, this little guest room is already starting to look like Tyler's room at our old house. Movie posters on the wall, drawings on the desk, clothes and shoes thrown all over. He's adjusted as if nothing has happened.

I reach over and touch Tyler on the forehead. He is asleep,

dreaming of little-boy things, like I used to dream before the world split in half. He still doesn't really understand about that. Good for him.

I climb into bed with him, pretending I'm him. Pretending I'm just a little boy worrying about broken Crayolas and whether first grade will be harder than kindergarten. I stroke his hair, like Dad used to stroke mine. I must be his daddy now. I must protect him from evil things.

Danny should have killed himself instead, I heard people mumble the night of the "accident," when everyone we knew invaded the house. They mumbled evil things when they thought Grandma and Grandpa couldn't hear. *He should die and burn in hell forever.*

I could believe them if I wanted to.

I could hate Dad like I hate the devil. Is that what Mom would do? Should I take Mom's side?

I could hate him, for Mom definitely did not deserve what he did to her—but then I look at Grandma. There is no hate in her toward anyone. How can she be that way? Is that normal? Is it right?

As I lie there, listening to the rain and to Tyler's quiet breathing, I realize that I don't ever have to side with my mother or my father ever again about anything. Now I can side with my grandparents. They will tell me what to do and how to feel.

They say they forgive Dad. And surely if Mom's parents can forgive the man who murdered her, then maybe I can, too.

8

A WALL OF GLASS

June

The jail is a terrible place. Below, the floor tiles don't quite reach the walls. Above, old pipes run along the ceiling, weaving in and out of rooms like snakes. It smells like my worst pair of Nikes, and the gray walls are sloppily painted. Those walls seem the worst thing of all. Whoever painted the walls didn't care about the job—they steamrolled gray paint over signs and thermostats, anything that got in the way. Little gray splatters of paint cover the fading black and white tiles of the floor. Nobody should live in a place where the painters didn't care.

There are police officers and guards everywhere, but still I don't feel safe. The iron bars are covered with the same gray paint, slopped on by the same miserable workers. A gate opens in front of us, and the guard closes it behind. Then another. I imagine I'm going through an air lock on a space-ship. The prison barge. I try to make believe it's all pretend.

We are led to a room, take a number, and then we wait and wait and wait.

Finally we are led to another gray room, divided in the middle by a long scratched-up counter and a thick glass wall that goes to the ceiling. It's like a big ticket booth at a movie theater in a bad part of town. On the other side of the glass are the inmates, talking on the phone to their visitors. How stupid, I think. They're just inches away, but they have to talk by phone.

Most of the inmates on the other side of the glass *look* like criminals. Most of the *visitors* look like criminals, too. I stay close by Grandma's side, not caring if I look like a wimp.

A guard leads Dad to the room on the other side of the glass, and Dad sits in a chair. He doesn't look at me. He pretends he doesn't know I'm there yet, but he knows.

This has been the longest I've ever been away from my dad. Three months. I figured he'd be in a wheelchair or something, or walk with an awful limp, on account of he shot himself, but he doesn't. He's healed.

Dad's long blond hair is cut short. He looks like he's lost even more weight. His eyes are sunken in farther than I've ever seen them, and there are dark rings around them.

He looks like a criminal, too.

Grandma goes to talk to him first. . . . Then Grandpa. . . .

Then they bring Tyler and me. I pick up the phone on my side of the wall, and Dad picks up his at the same time. Like two sides of a mirror.

"Hi, Preston," he says. "How are you?"

"Fine." I don't tell him that I have nightmares.

"How's school?"

"Fine." I don't tell him that my friends treat me like I'm from another planet.

"How's everything?"

"Fine."

He nods.

"I missed a few weeks, but my grades are back up," I tell him. "They even let me stay on the track team." That seems to make him happy.

"Have you won lots of races?"

"Most of 'em," I say with a shrug. "Maybe Grandpa could take pictures for you at our next meet," I tell him. I don't tell him that the season's over and there won't be any more meets.

I look at him closely through the reinforced glass. I sort of wish I could hug him, but in a way I'm glad the glass is there. But I can't tell him that. Used to be I could tell my dad anything.

"Pictures," says Dad, "pictures would be nice."

I suddenly realize I can't think of anything to say. I get scared. Real scared. I turn to see Grandma and Grandpa standing behind me. They just smile at me, like this is the most wonderful moment in the world. It makes me feel better. If they think this is wonderful, then maybe it is.

I turn back to Dad. "Do they feed you good?"

"Oh, yeah," he says. "Every day's Thanksgiving." I laugh at his joke even though it's not all that funny.

"Hey," says Tyler, "gimme a chance. I wanna talk to him, too." Tyler grabs the phone away from me, and I grab it back.

"You don't grab things!" I tell him. "Ask nicely. Use the *p* word."

Tyler sighs. "Can I *please* talk to Dad now?"

"Much better." I hand him the phone, and he steps up to the glass. He's so small his head barely clears the little ledge in the booth. Dad looks down on him with his sunken eyes.

"You like it here?" asks Tyler.

"It's okay," Dad says.

"You get your own room?" asks Tyler.

"I share it," Dad says.

"Bunk beds?"

Dad nods.

"Who do you share it with?"

"A guy named Bob."

Tyler nods and wrinkles his brow, trying to picture what a guy named Bob might look like.

"Can I see your room?"

Dad shakes his head.

"Oh," says Tyler, a bit disappointed.

"I miss you, Tyler," says Dad.

"Me too," says Tyler. "Why did you kill my mommy?"

I instantly bodycheck Tyler against the wall and grab the phone away from him. Tyler whines and complains, but I push him back behind me.

"What?" says Dad. "What was that? What, Tyler?" He pretends he didn't hear. But he heard. I know he heard, and he knows that I know he heard. But we play the game. We both pretend.

"Are you coming out soon?" I ask him.

He shakes his head. "I still have to go to trial."

"Oh."

Behind me Tyler is sniffling, more upset about the way I pushed him out of the way than anything else.

"Dad," I ask, looking at his eyes, trying to see if they're the same eyes I remembered, "are you better now?"

"I'm feeling okay," he says, rubbing his stomach just above his belly button.

"No," I say, clearly and slowly. "I mean are you *better* now?"

He looks at me for a moment, then looks down and starts picking at his fingernails.

"Preston," he says. "I love you, Preston. And I'm sorry." He starts to cry. "I'm sorry I'm sorry I'm sorry."

And that's about enough. I turn around and give the phone to Grandma. I will not cry. I will not cry now. All these criminals looking at me, all these stone-faced guards. I give the phone to Grandma, and she talks to Dad. She cries a bit and calms him down. She's good with people who cry. She should be a professional grandmother.

I lean back against the ugly gray wall. It's sticky even though the paint has probably been dry for years and years. I stand back, close my eyes, and force down the tears so the criminals won't see, and I count the minutes until we can get out of this awful place and go home.

9

SECRET PLACES

September

There is nothing but the football field now. That's the way I like it. My uniform pads me against the tackling force of the other team; the cheering people standing on the sidelines pad me against the outside world. And now, there is nothing but the field.

I'm almost twelve, but I feel much older in my uniform. My shoulders seem to stretch out a mile on both sides. The quarterback yells "set," and I dig my cleats into the sod, ram my knuckles into the ground. I feel as hard and stable as a rock when I get down into position, but I feel as fast and light as a tiger when I run.

The kid facing me on the other team is too slow, and we both know it. We both know I'll be sailing far away from him the instant the ball is snapped. He can't cover me. No one can.

The center snaps the ball to the quarterback, and I leave the jumble of bodies and helmets far behind. In front of me, there's nothing but the field. I am a rocket blasting out of orbit, and my cleats burn grass as I go. I will not turn around until I am in the end zone.

A bigger kid from the other team comes up alongside me, like a missile trying to take me out—but he knows he can't touch me until I have the ball. He runs just beside me, so I activate my second stage and roar on ahead, leaving him in smoke. I am in orbit, and it's beautiful. The most perfect feeling in the world—having nothing to think about but the field. This is *my* quilt. Grandma has hers; this is mine.

I am in the end zone. I am alone. And I turn. The ball is already spiraling in the air toward me. Almost toward me— it's off to my right. Reflexively, I dig my cleats into the end zone and push off to the right. The field is gone. Now there is nothing but the ball. It seems to fly at me in slow motion, spinning closer and closer. I watch it dock smoothly and cleanly in my hands. I feel the lace and the rough imitation pigskin against the balls of my fingers. I clamp down tight, and the ball is mine.

Now there is nothing but me.

Holding the ball close, I dive, then roll on the hard, damp earth—not because I have to, but because I want to. I want to feel my body slamming down, hard enough to sting but not hard enough to hurt. I want to scream for joy at the top of my lungs until I have no voice. I want to enjoy this moment, and I want it to go on forever and ever.

I am the fastest!

I am the strongest!

I am . . .

Weavin' Warren Sharp?

With that thought, the world rushes back in on me with the tackling force of the entire NFL. Grandma and Grandpa watch from the side cheering. My teammates race to me, trying to lift me onto their shoulders.

But all that doesn't matter. The good feeling is gone.

Grandpa holds a camera, taking pictures. For Dad. This is the first touchdown I've ever made that Dad wasn't here to see. That Mom wasn't here to see. And although I am the center of attention—although I've put our team in the lead—the play is over, and the smile on my face is only there to mask what I'm feeling inside. It's the feeling that something is missing—like all my guts, or my brains, or my heart. Or my soul. My hands can catch footballs fine, but they can't do what I really want them to do. I want them to reach inside my body. I want to use my fists to fill that empty space inside, wherever it is.

"Yeah, Preston!" scream my friends and teammates while the other team takes a walk down the field. "You'll be MVP for sure."

Yes, I will be. I will push harder than I've pushed for

anything. I will make that happen. I *have* to make it happen. For Mom.

I close my eyes, take a few deep breaths, and make the outside world go away again. The hold inside that my hands can't reach is hidden once more. I push it back, until it is forgotten. I step forward into the kickoff formation and open my eyes.

In a moment there will be nothing but the field. Good. That's the way I like it.

We moved in July—my grandparents, Tyler, and I—to a brand-new house in a richer neighborhood. The town we moved to is one of those places that's perfectly planned from the day they started building it. The place seems to be trying so hard to be normal, it's just plain weird. All the homes look different, but somehow they all look the same. The grass is always green and as well-trimmed as a golf course—the parks all seem too pretty to be used—and right smack in the middle of town is this huge man-made lake, filled with water that's always dyed a little bit too blue.

This town is like Disneyland without the rides.

Our house is big. We have four bedrooms upstairs, and downstairs there's a sunken living room, a raised den, and a dining room that sort of floats in between.

My room isn't a guest room. It's *my* room. It looks like my room; it feels like my room. It even has my old bed in it.

Grandma tucks me in at night now, like Mom used to. I

don't really need to be tucked in, but I let her do it because I know grandmas love that stuff. Letting her tuck me in is the least I can do.

Grandpa does all the things a dad should do, but he's not as strict about it as my dad might be. Sometimes I even slip and call him Dad by mistake. He just smiles when I do that. Grandma and Grandpa like having us around. I like having them around. It's a good arrangement.

And they never fight.

Life is calm, and life is normal. Of course it's also sort of plain—like the iced tea Grandma always has in the fridge. Weak with no sugar. But maybe that's what life is supposed to be like.

I seem to spend a lot of time on the football field, either at practice or in games. When I'm off the field, I spend a lot of time behind my closet.

Whoever built the house must have had me in mind when they built it, because there's a secret sliding door at the back of my closet, and beyond that door is a secret room, only five feet high. It's my place, and very few people are allowed in. I have a TV in there, and there are some pillows and chairs to sit on when I have friends over, but mostly I sit there alone. Grandma doesn't come in. It's as if, just because it's behind a closet, she feels funny crossing the threshold, so she just tells me to keep it clean and lets me sweep and vacuum the hard plywood floor all by myself.

It's a good place to disappear.

I sometimes pretend that time stops when I sit in there. Now that the trial is coming up, I pretend more and more.

"What trial?" asks my friend Jason as we sit in the secret room. I don't answer him right away. I met Jason when I first started at my new school. The first day I met him, we played pool at his house. He hit the cue ball too hard—it went flying off the table and hit me in the nuts. When a friendship starts that way, it can only get better. "What trial?" he asks again.

"Just some dumb old trial," I say, hoping he'll back off. Jason doesn't know. None of my new friends know. I think it's one of the reasons why my grandparents decided to move. To give me a new school, new friends. I left everyone behind—I don't write or call any of my old friends now. I thought I might when I left. I told people I would, but the truth is I get all sweaty when I think about talking to them again. As far as I'm concerned, I hope I never hear from any of them ever again.

Especially not Russ Talbert.

It was Russ's parents who lent my dad the gun.

I don't know why, and I don't want to know why. I hate Russ. He always talked about how great separation and divorce was—and then *his* parents end up getting back together.

"What dumb old trial?" Jason's the type of guy who has to know everything—and remembers everything he hears. He's pretty smart, and although he's not as good in football or track as I am, we make a good team. Although we look like opposites—him with his dark, dark brown hair and me with my light, light blond hair.

"I said, what dumb old trial?" he asks impatiently.

"Nothing," I say. "Just my dad's trial, so shut up!"

I want to hit him. I want to hit him so hard he'll shut up. I can feel my temper about to explode like a gunshot. Jason's eyes light up. "Cool! Your father's on trial for something?"

"There's nothing cool about it," I tell him, clenching my fists, wishing that I was here in my secret room alone today.

"What'd he do? Rob a bank? Steal a car? Or did he just embezzle or something?"

I look down. "He killed someone."

"No way!" says Jason, both excited and horrified. "You're making this up. You're just trying to trick me."

"Right," I say, "it's a trick. So shut up."

But he doesn't shut up. Even though he's only known me a short time, he knows me better than any of my old friends did. He sees my fists clenched silently by my side, my knuckles white.

Jason knows that I'm telling him the truth, even though I'd prefer he thought I was lying.

"Who'd he kill?" asks Jason, almost in a whisper. "Anybody important?"

I shrug. "Just my mom."

His eyes widen, but just a little. He purses his lips, first nodding in understanding, then shaking his head with a sigh.

"That sucks," he says, and he says it with the authority of someone who really knows what sucks and what doesn't. It's not like the wishy-washy nervous little things my old friends used to say before they all ran away from being my friends. "That sucks." Yeah, he's right. It does. It's about time someone put it so plainly and simply.

Jason leans back against the wall and looks up to the five-foot ceiling of the secret room—only he's not really looking there, he's thinking about something. My fists unclench all by themselves.

"You know," he says, "I lost my mom, too."

"No!" But even as I say it, I realize that I never have seen his mother, just his dad. He never talks about his mother either. Just like me.

"She's not dead," he says, "but she did leave my dad, my brothers, and me when I was really little."

"I'm sorry," I say, wondering why people say they're sorry when it wasn't even their fault. I feel genuinely bad about it—even though I usually get mad when people think of divorce as being anything like what happened to me. Jason accepts the apology with a nod.

"I tell everyone else that it was just a plain old simple divorce," he says in a whisper that anywhere else in the house would be too quiet to even hear. "But it's worse than that. She moved to Arizona." Then he looks up at me. "You're the first person I've really told."

"I won't tell," I assure him, matching his whisper, so that no one else but the shirts and pants hanging in the closet can hear.

"Neither will I," he whispers back.

It's the very next day, while Jason and I are riding our bikes home from school, that we run into Angela. She's walking home in front of us, and when we see her, we slow down, then get off our bikes and walk them, keeping way behind her on this bicycle path that winds around the lake.

It's only a few weeks into the school year, so there are lots of kids I still don't know. Angela is one of them. There are no Prestonettes hanging outside my door anymore, like they did at my old house. It's too bad, because now that I'm starting to finally get interested in girls, I barely know any of them.

"I know from a reliable source," says Jason, "that Angela likes you."

"Naah, get outta here!" I wave it off but want to hear more. We round a turn and slowly follow her as she walks up the wooden footbridge that crosses the too-blue lake.

She stops halfway across and looks over the side into the water. I wonder whether she's just doing it to do it or if she's trying to stall until we reach her.

"Uh-oh!" says Jason. "What do we do now?"

"Just keep walking," I say.

We walk our bikes up to her. I'm about to walk past, but

then pretend to just notice her for the first time. "Oh—hi!" I say.

"Hi," she says.

"You're Angela, right?"

"M-hmm."

"Hi, I'm Preston." I shake her hand. "This is Jason." She shakes his hand, and then she turns to look out into the water.

"Will you look at that?" she says, pointing. "Those are the largest koi fish I've ever seen in my life!"

Beneath the surface of the water, I see about six mutant goldfish swimming into what looks like a current of water being pumped into the lake.

"Man, those are *huge!*" I look at Angela again. "You live around here?"

She points. "One of those condos on the lake."

"That's not far," I say, and offer for Jason and me to walk her home.

On the way, Angela talks a lot—as if she's been waiting a long time to talk to someone. It's fine with me. The more she talks, the less I have to. She goes on about her house, and her brother, and her parents, and how her father writes computer programs for NASA, and how her mother is a big-time realtor. And then, just as we near her house, she asks the question.

"What about *your* parents? What do they do?"

"I live with my grandparents," I tell her. "My grandfather's a high-school coach. My grandmother teaches piano."

"Why don't you live with your parents?" she asks.

Jason, who has acted kind of like a third wheel since we left the bridge, completely seals his mouth and watches us, his eyes darting back and forth from Angela to me. Angela notices.

"Is there . . . something the matter with them?"

"Nothing's the matter with them. It's just that they're out of the country," I say, amazed at how easily the lie comes. "They travel a lot."

Jason picks up from there. "Yeah," he says. "I've never even met them either. They're always in Europe or something."

Angela smiles and accepts this without a second thought. She goes on to tell all about her parents' trip to Europe.

And as Angela waves and hurries off into her house, something becomes very clear to me.

Even if Angela ends up being my first official girlfriend, she will never know about that terrible Thursday last March and the reason I live with my grandparents. No one in this too-perfect town except for Jason has to know, and no one will. No one.

10

TURKEY IN HEAVEN

November

I would have skipped Thanksgiving if I had a choice, but I don't.

"There's nothing to be thankful for," I told Grandma and Grandpa, but of course they disagreed, and Grandma came up with a long list of all the things that I personally ought to be thankful for. My grandma's incredible that way. She could see the bright side of a black hole. Grandpa says some people see a glass of water as half full, others see it as half empty, and Grandma sees it as a whole pitcher of lemonade.

And so we have a big Thanksgiving family dinner, minus two, and everybody pretends that nothing is wrong.

Everyone's there by noon. Only relatives. I used to have friends over for Thanksgiving, but not this year. Angela wanted to come over for part of the day, so I told her Tyler had the chicken pox.

In the kitchen, Grandma is kept company by Aunt Jackie and Uncle Steve. Her two remaining children. Mom would be cooking, too, if she were here. She'd be making yams with little marshmallows. She'd be making homemade cranberry sauce and twice-baked potatoes.

Aunt Jackie and Grandma baste the turkey, which has been in the oven for hours already. Uncle Steve stands around the kitchen picking crust from the pumpkin pies.

The huge turkey is still pale, but the air smells like Thanksgiving. I wish it didn't, because it doesn't *feel* like Thanksgiving.

"The last time I cooked a turkey," says Aunt Jackie, "it—" Then Aunt Jackie cuts herself short, stopping in the middle of the sentence.

"It what?" I ask.

Grandma closes the oven and checks the temperature. She pretends not to hear.

"It what?" I ask again.

"It burned," says Jackie. "That's all, it just burned."

"Why'd you let it burn?"

Uncle Steve puts down the pumpkin pie and walks out of the room. I suddenly realize I've hit some sort of motherlode, but it's too late to shut up now.

"It was the day of the 'accident,'" Aunt Jackie finally says. "I had a turkey cooking. I ended up leaving it in there for three days. Nothing was left of it when I finally got home, the poor thing."

She laughs a little. Grandma laughs a little. Then Aunt Jackie cries, like you cry when you laugh too hard—but she wasn't laughing too hard. "That poor old turkey," she says again, drying her damp eyes. And then she hugs me for no reason. There's lots of hugging for no reason going on today.

Out back Tyler plays a game of touch football with our cousins, most of whom are closer to his age. As I watch them, Uncle Steve sneaks up behind me, picks me up, tosses me around, and wrestles. I refuse to enjoy it, and tell him to quit, but he doesn't. He keeps it up until I laugh in spite of myself. He spins me by my arms, drops me to the ground, and then yells at Tyler and the others for roughhousing. I sneak back inside.

Later everyone sits in the living room, waiting for dinner to be ready.

"Remember the time," says Aunt Jackie, munching on chips and dip in the living room, "Megan won the Miss Bank of America beauty contest?" She smiles and thinks back.

"She was so happy," says Grandpa. "Remember how we all sang to her 'There she is, Miss Bank-of-America'?"

On TV, the game is into its second quarter. The smell of Thanksgiving is so strong, it makes me feel like I'm seven, and the four of us are going to Grandma and Grandpa's old house, when Thanksgiving was much more fun.

"Remember your slumber parties?" says Grandma to Aunt Jackie. "You were so mean to your friends!" Aunt Jackie laughs and covers her face, knowing what's coming. Grandma turns to everyone else. "Jackie and Megan would always wake up before their friends did in the morning, and they would decorate their sleeping friends' faces with whipped cream and raisins and sprinkles, and then they would stick big ribbon bows on their foreheads!"

Everyone laughs except for Uncle Steve. He turns up the television volume with the remote control.

"Remember the time—"

"Can we please not talk about this?" says Uncle Steve. "It's supposed to be Thanksgiving." No one but the sportscasters answers back.

"There's nothing wrong with talking about Megan, Steve," says Grandpa.

"Can't we just watch football in peace?"

"Steve," says Aunt Jackie. "Do you remember when we used to call you Piggy Poodle?"

Everyone but Steve laughs. He shakes his head and turns up the volume. Uncle Steve hasn't stopped being angry since the "accident." When Mom died he didn't have Grandma's Peace.

Thinking quickly, I change the subject.

"Dad's trial's coming up soon," I say, "isn't it?"

It's like a boulder falls from the sky and shatters Grandma's glass coffee table. Everyone takes a deep breath and shifts uncomfortably in their seats. Maybe I didn't change the subject enough.

"I'll check on that turkey," says Uncle Steve, and he makes a quick exit into the kitchen. His wife, Aunt Linda, goes after him.

"I hate football," says one of my little cousins.

In my secret room Tyler and I watch the end of the game together. I usually don't let him in here, but today is an exception. There are so many people in the house, there's nowhere else he can go to escape. Keeping him out would be cruel and unusual punishment.

"Do you think," asks Tyler, "that they cook turkeys in heaven?"

"Naah," I answer him. "They don't need turkeys there."

"Then what do they eat on Thanksgiving?"

"You don't eat in heaven," I tell him.

"That's no fun," he says.

"It is *too* fun," I tell him. "Heaven's so much fun that you don't even have time to eat. You don't care about eating anymore."

Tyler wrinkles his brow and thinks about this. "But if they *did* have turkeys," he asks, "do you think Mom would cook one? Or would she be eating one in someone else's house?"

"Okay, Tyler," I say, thinking this one through. "If there were turkeys in heaven—I'm not saying there are—but if there were, Mom wouldn't have to cook it. Jesus cooks it—he cooks one humongous turkey, and it's enough to feed everyone in heaven, like he fed the five thousand with the five loaves of bread."

"Oh," says Tyler.

Behind me I hear the closet door slide open, and the shirts and pants begin to rustle clumsily.

"Hello in there!" Uncle Steve pokes his head in, knocking down some hangers in the closet. "This is your hangout?"

"Sometimes," I tell him.

"Can I come in?"

"Kids only," I tell him.

"Oh, I see."

Uncle Steve stands there in the closet for a moment, just on the threshold of the secret room, fiddling with his mustache.

"Listen," he finally says. "I just wanted to say I'm sorry if I upset you there in the living room."

"Didn't upset me," I say. I keep my eyes on the game, never looking at Uncle Steve.

"Yeah . . . well, I'm sorry."

He sort of hangs there for a minute like the shirts and pants. I still don't look at him.

"We'll be eating any minute," he says.

"I had too many chips," I tell him. "I'll eat the leftovers. It's okay."

He hangs for a few more seconds, then leaves.

"Close the door!" I yell after him. I hear the closet door sliding shut.

"But I'm hungry," says Tyler.

"So get out of here."

Tyler fiddles with his shoelaces and pokes his nose, but he doesn't leave. I'm glad he doesn't.

"Why didn't you let Uncle Steve in here?" he asks. "Don't you like him?"

"Of course I like him," I tell Tyler. "It's just that he doesn't forgive Dad, like the rest of us do. Nobody who doesn't forgive Dad is allowed in here."

"Does he hate Dad?" asks Tyler.

"How should I know?" I answer.

Tyler stands up and plants his foot against the wall in a slow-motion ninja kick. It leaves a big black footprint. "If Uncle Steve hates Dad, then I hate Uncle Steve."

"You *can't* hate him," I explain to Tyler. "He's your uncle—you have to love him, no matter what he thinks."

"Well, then, I *do* love Uncle Steve," says Tyler. "I love him, but I hate him, too."

"You can't love *and* hate someone," I explain to him.

"Why not?"

"Because that's just the way it is."

Tyler plants another footprint on the wall, making a matching pair, and then he turns to me.

"You don't know everything," he says.

11

ON MY SHOULDERS

December

I know the gray walls of the jailhouse now. They are my friends. In the frozen dribbles of paint, I can see sloppy, pockmarked faces escorting me down the long halls and through the "air lock" gates. The same faces stand peeling behind me and keep me company when I wait and wait to speak with my dad. If walls could talk, they would whisper "hello" and call me by name.

The talk at home is all about Dad's trial, but the talk is always over my head and behind my back, so I don't know too much. To me, Dad's trial hangs in front of us like the moon above the freeway. You can keep driving toward it, but it never seems to get any closer. It's supposed to happen soon, but nobody tells me when—and when it happens, Dad's entire life will be decided for him. Prison for a few years.

Prison for life. Could they even give him the death penalty? I don't ask anyone because I'm afraid of the answer.

"Are you scared about it?" I ask my dad on the smelly jailhouse phone that connects one side of the glass to the other.

Dad looks down. "A little," he says.

"Don't be," I tell him. "Grandma and Grandpa Pearson won't let you go to prison."

"It's not up to them, Preston," he says. He thinks for a moment, then says, in his fatherly lecture sort of way, "I did something wrong. And when you do something wrong, you have to pay." He says it like he's trying to teach me not to steal candy from the store. Why does he try to make it seem so simple? Does he really think of it that way, or is it just that he thinks *I* think that way?

"I'm not Tyler, Dad," I tell him. "You don't have to tell me about right and wrong. I'm twelve, remember?"

"You are, aren't you." He turns his cheek, like I slapped him in his face. "I wish I could have been there for your birthday," he told me. "Did you like the bike?"

"Yeah," I say. I don't want to talk about my birthday. It wasn't much fun.

"Did Grandpa pick out a nice one?" he asks.

"Yeah," I say. "A blue ten-speed. Grandpa has pictures."

"Someday, Preston," he tells me, "I'll get you a dirt bike— would you like that?"

"Yeah!" I say.

"The best one they make," he tells me. "You can ride it all around town—show off to your friends at school. How does that sound?"

"Sounds great!"

"Maybe I'll get one, too," he says. He looks through the glass, but he doesn't seem to see me. It's as if the glass is a window into some other time—years from now maybe. Open fields and dirt bikes. Him riding with me. Best friends, like we used to be. "Wouldn't that be something?" he says.

"Yeah, it would be."

He puts up his hand to the glass and presses his fingers against it. It's kind of silly, but it's better than nothing. It's the closest thing to a hug we can get. I wonder who needs the hug more, him or me. I put my hand against his on the glass, holding it there like a high five, but I take my hand away before he does.

"When I get out, we can do stuff like that, Preston."

But that's only *if* he gets out. For all I know, putting my hand against the glass is the closest I'll ever come to hugging him again.

"How soon could you get out?"

He takes his time answering. "It depends on the trial," he says, and we both know what that means. It means he may never get out. The Talberts—Russ's parents—are testifying against him. Even though they told my grandparents to their faces that they love my dad, they're testifying against him, telling how Dad tricked Mr. Talbert into lending him the gun.

Grandma and Grandpa are testifying *for* my dad. Dad's lawyer thinks that if they testify, explaining how they've known him since he was fifteen and know he's a good person—how they felt that both he and Mom were terribly disturbed, and that they still love him—then maybe a jury would let him off easy. But as much as I like the idea of Dad getting off, it still bothers me.

Just because he was disturbed and people still love him doesn't necessarily mean it's *right* for him to get out of jail. I'm sure lots of people in prison for life, or even on death row, were disturbed when they committed their crimes. I'm sure that most of them have people who love them, too. And the only difference is that this one happens to be my dad.

Tyler impatiently reaches up to grab the phone from me. He uses the *p* word, so I have to give it to him.

"I love you, Preston," says my father before I hand over the phone.

"Yeah, Dad," I say. "I love you, too."

January

My secret room has no windows, so I don't know if it's dark yet. They say the days have started to get longer now that it's January, but I haven't seen it. The sun still sets by five. The days are getting colder—not cold enough for snow, but cold enough to make you wish you didn't have to get out of bed. It's probably about five now. I study science while Jason organizes my entire baseball-card collection in some mysterious but brilliant filing system. Jason never seems to study. We're both good students, but he's a good student by nature. I, on the other hand, have to study my butt off. We sort of have a competition going—you know?—who can pull in higher grades. He always wins, but not by much.

Today science seems to bypass my brain completely. I sigh and slam down the textbook.

"What's your problem?" asks Jason.

"I've just been wondering something," I tell him.

"About science?"

"No, about life, and God and stuff."

"Oh, one of *those* questions," he says rolling his eyes. "You think about God and stuff more than anyone I know our age."

He's right about that, and I'm kind of glad about it. I guess it's because my grandparents are really strict about going to church and things like that. That must be the reason.

"I'm just wondering," I tell him, "if someone helps a murderer get out of prison, do you think they're damned?"

Jason takes the question very seriously. He thinks about it, then answers me. He doesn't answer the question I actually asked—but instead answers the question I was afraid to ask.

"I don't think you'll be damned if you testify for your father, Preston," he says. "I don't see how you could be."

Grandma doesn't want me to testify; she thinks it'll be too traumatic. Maybe it will be, but Dad's lawyer thinks I should because if Dad's found guilty of first-degree murder, "the judge will have no mercy." He could be in prison for life, or worse.

"Preston's testimony," the lawyer said, "could make all the difference in the world." I haven't told Dad that I might testify. I don't have the guts to tell him that the rest of his life rests on my shoulders. But I think he already knows.

"If all you're doing," says Jason, "is telling the truth, then I don't see how you could be damned."

"But what if my dad doesn't deserve to go free?" I say.

"But what if he planned what he did ahead of time?"

"What if he was nuts when he did it?"

"But what if he knew exactly what he was doing?"

"But what if he really can't remember doing it, like he says?"

I give up. Jason plays Ping-Pong with words much better than I play Ping-Pong with paddles—and while I could always whip Russ Talbert on a table, Jason wins with words every time.

"Listen," says Jason, "you know your dad; I don't. I mean, do you really think he'd ever kill anyone in cold blood?"

"No . . . but he did."

Jason has no answer to that one. For once, I really wish he did.

"Maybe it wasn't really in cold blood," I offer. "Maybe it was just in warm blood."

"Maybe."

I open my science book to an impossibly confused diagram of the insides of a frog. Tomorrow we dissect. I try to figure which is harder to understand: the impossible insides of a frog, or my father.

"Listen, the way I figure it, it's a coin toss," says Jason. "Heads: your dad was nuts, is better now, and deserves a second chance. Or tails: he knew what he was doing, did it anyway, and deserves the worst. And since you really don't know whether it's heads or tails, you might as well testify, because all you'll be telling is the truth."

"But he killed someone," I say, slamming my book on the impossible frog. "What happens if he's set free because I testify?"

"Yeah," says Jason, "but what happens if he gets the electric chair because you don't?"

Just the thought of it puts me in my own little electric chair for a split second, stopping my heart and starting it with a bang that pushes out on the insides of my chest. But hearing Jason put it so clearly, as he tends to do, makes my own choice very clear. It makes me realize that I have no choice. I have to testify.

"Mom must hate me by now," I say, but Jason says nothing. Maybe he didn't hear me. Or maybe he just agrees.

Thursday, January 24

The courtroom is not what I imagined. It doesn't look as clean as I thought it would. It doesn't look as old.

The room is empty as the bailiff leads me and my grandma down the aisle toward the judge. She has already testified. So has Grandpa. I'm the only one left. It's as if I'm walking into the middle of someone else's nightmare. I don't know what went on before I got here; I don't know what happens after I leave. It's been going on for weeks and may go on for weeks more. I try to tell myself that my tiny time on the stand is only a small, unimportant part of the whole trial, but as I walk into the courtroom, I can't help but feel that my tiny time on the stand *is* the whole trial.

The jury isn't here. Neither are the Talberts or anyone else.

Dad isn't here either. I asked for that. I couldn't testify in front of him. I can't even mention Mom in front of him. If he were here, I would just die right there on the witness stand. And so it's just me and the judge and Grandma.

But it's not, is it?

I know God is there, too. I know Mom is there. And I'm scared.

"Preston," says the judge. "I want you to listen to each question carefully and answer to the best of your ability. Take as much time as you need—don't let anyone make you feel rushed."

I nod my head quickly, like a scared rabbit. I'm glad no one else is here—I probably look real stupid. They'd probably laugh. All my friends would laugh. They'd laugh because I'm shaking. They'd laugh because my grandmother is on the other side of me holding my hand. The funny thing is, I need her to be there. I'd probably pass out or something if she wasn't. Does that make me a wimp?

I try to calm myself by thinking of good things. Football. My MVP trophy. I stood up there real proud and strong when I accepted that trophy. Why can't I do that now? Why? "This is for my mom," I said when I got the trophy. It made Grandma and Grandpa cry. Why can't I stop shaking?

"Okay, Preston," says Mr. Hendricks, Dad's lawyer, as he begins his questioning. I know what he's going to ask—we went over it before.

"Nothing to it," Mr. Hendricks said when he was at our house the other day. "It's just like taking a test when you've been given all the answers."

The trick, Mr. Hendricks explained, was to be *sure* of my answers and never go back on anything that I say. So we talked, and I thought back to everything that happened those weeks before Dad did what he did. I thought back, and I remembered a lot more than I thought I did. I remembered that day Dad and I rented the house by the beach—the one we never got to move into. How we visited the school I never got to go to. How he bought me that wetsuit I never got to wear. I returned the wetsuit to the store after Mom died. I went to return the key to the owner of the house.

I remembered their last fight. Money. Mom buys too many clothes. We can't make the house payments. Dad only makes a few thousand dollars a month. Sounds like a lot to me, but compared to Aunt Jackie's ex-husband, it's nothing.

I remembered Mom yelling to Dad about me—how she just didn't have the patience for me anymore.

I remembered how she bragged about Weavin' Warren Sharp to my father, knowing that Dad was super-jealous and would make more of the whole thing than it probably was.

I remembered Dad talking to Mr. Talbert about his gun. That was even months before it happened—Dad wanted to buy a gun for Mom's protection when he wasn't home. He wanted the same gun Mr. Talbert had, and Dad went out shopping with him.

But Mom didn't want one. She was afraid of guns, so Dad never bought it.

And so, as I sit up on the witness stand, Mr. Hendricks asks me all the questions he said he would, and I answer them as best I can, even though I shake and even though my tongue doesn't want to move in my mouth.

If this is the easy stuff, I can't wait till the hard stuff.

"The district attorney," said Mr. Hendricks the other day, "will question you after I do—almost the same questions, but he'll try to confuse you and frighten you. Remember to stick to what you know, and don't let him rattle you." But that's only if Mr. Hendricks ever finishes questioning me, and he seems to be taking forever. Finally he begins to wind down.

"One more question," says Mr. Hendricks before he backs away. He hesitates and looks me straight in the eye.

"Do you want your father back, Preston?"

He keeps looking right into my eyes. The judge waits for me to answer. He didn't tell me he'd ask this one! He didn't warn me! My eyes start to fill with tears. *No fair!* I want to yell. *No fair!*

Do I want my father back? Dad did something horrible. Something that no father should ever do for any reason. He shot my mom in the back of the head. That should matter—it has to matter, but somehow it doesn't. He's my dad. My only dad. And even if Mom hates me for it, I can't lie, I just can't. Do I want my father back?

"Yes," I say, losing control. "I want him back. I want him to come home." Sobbing, I turn my eyes away from Mr. Hendricks and the judge. He tricked me! He wasn't supposed to make me do this. He wasn't!

I close my eyes tight and try to stop the tears, but they don't stop. Grandma squeezes my hand tightly.

"Your witness," says Mr. Hendricks to the mean-looking district attorney, who stands there waiting for me to stop crying.

12

BETWEEN THE LINES

March—One Year Later

Twenty-four pictures that Grandpa took sit on my desk. I look at each one of them. Me running down the field. Me catching a pass. Me being lifted up by my teammates. One of Tyler, quietly watching on the sidelines with Grandma.

Football season's been over for months now, but the pictures have been on a shelf all this time.

And Dad's in prison.

I grab a piece of paper from the drawer and begin writing.

Dear Dad,

And then I stop. What do you say to your dad in a letter? When he was in jail, we visited him almost every Sunday, so I never had to write, but now he's farther away. We only get to visit once a month or so.

Dear Dad,
Hi. How are you?

He's looking much better these days. He's finally putting back on some of the weight he lost. His eyes aren't so sunken in. He smiles every once in a while, and sometimes it even seems like he's not forcing it. "His countenance is pleasant," as my grandmother would say. Prison's a lot better for him than jail was. It's better for us, too. It's bigger—there's more open space. There's a big yard there, with a high fence, and guard towers, but you can walk in there, and run and exercise.

Most important, there's no glass between us. When we visit, I get to hug my dad now.

We're all fine. Well, actually Tyler has a cold and I
caught it from him but don't worry, it's not too bad.
Grandma gives us soup and tea all the time. I'm sick
of soup and tea.

Dad was never convicted. The jury found him innocent of both first-degree murder and second-degree murder, and they were hung on the manslaughter charge. They just couldn't make up their minds.

The district attorney could have charged him again for manslaughter, and Dad would have gone to trial again, with a new jury, but instead he cut a deal with Dad's lawyer. Dad goes to prison for five years. That's a lot better than life. It's a lot better than death row.

Bet you're already counting the days till you get out. I know I am. Anyway, five years isn't that long.

But it is long. It's sixty months. It's 1,825 days—26 if you count leap year. It's 43,824 hours. I know all this because I figured it out. I know it down to the seconds. Five years means we'll have a new president. It means I'll be graduating high school. It means a whole lifetime, to me. Even if they count the time he's already spent in jail, which I think they might, it will still seem like forever.

You're probably better off anyway—most kids hate their parents when they're like fourteen and fifteen, right? But you won't be around for me to hate, so you'll miss all that bad stuff.

Grandma keeps reminding me that there are lots of people who do fine without their parents, and aren't I lucky that so many people love me? There are lots of people who aren't loved at all. Street people. Abandoned kids. There are babies in Ethiopia covered with flies and starving to death. There was World War II. Whole families were wiped out because of what they believed. There was

Vietnam. Boys just a few years older than me got blown away, halfway around the world in a war they didn't even want to fight.

On the one-to-ten scale of lousiness, I would say what happened to me ranks only about a five. I shouldn't complain, but I do.

Maybe you can get out early for good behavior. So you'd better behave!

Uncle Steve complains more than I do. He doesn't say it very loud, but he says it. He feels it. We don't see him much anymore, and I don't know whether that's our fault or his. We all know that he would have testified against my dad if he had something to say and if he didn't respect my grandparents so much. He thinks we're all crazy for even talking to Dad after what he did.

Take good care of yourself, Dad. Don't get into prison riots or anything . . . and remember to eat all of your vegetables (ha-ha).

Maybe we *are* crazy, but I don't care.

We all miss you. We all can't wait to see you again. Love, your son, Preston

One thing gets stuck in my head, though. It was what the district attorney said. The D.A. was an evil little man, filled with hate, and when the verdict came down "not guilty," he pulled my grandmother aside and looked her in the eye.

"I hope you know that because of what you've done," he said to her, "your daughter is rolling over in her grave."

Grandma's face must have become hard and cold. Grandpa should have slugged him, but he didn't.

"You didn't even know our daughter," Grandpa said, returning the evil man's evil gaze. "You don't know Danny, either." And he led Grandma out of the courthouse.

Rolling over in her grave.

When I heard about it I got nightmares again. The closet. Other ones I'm too afraid to remember. Maybe ones I'm not supposed to remember.

"Grandma," I asked the next day, "if we forgive Dad, do you think Mom has forgiven Dad, too?"

She stopped playing the piano for a moment and looked at me as if she were amazed that such a thought could come from me.

"Yes, Preston," she finally said. "Of course she forgives him." Then she returned to playing.

The answer made me mad. It was the only time I can remember being mad at Grandma Lorraine. Not because of what she said, but because of the way she said it. As if she talked with Mom regularly by phone.

"But how do you *know*?" I asked her.

Still playing the piano, she answered calmly. "Because she's with God, Preston, and God *is* forgiveness. Forgiveness and love."

"But how can you be *sure* about it?"

She missed a note and pounded her hands on the keys in frustration. The grand piano let out a groan that lingered in the air.

"Stop asking that, Preston," she said, her infinite patience suddenly not as infinite as I'd thought. "Just stop asking that. There's no reason to. No reason at all!"

She rearranged her fingers on the piano and began to play again. Something soothing. Something beautiful and sacred. The slight redness in her face quickly faded away. As I watched her, I could imagine her playing the organ at her old church, many years ago. How beautiful her music is. How many other lost souls—kids and grown-ups—have heard her music in the street, walked into her church, and been saved through her music, the way she was saved through someone else's?

When you're sitting at the organ like that, so close to the pulpit and the preacher, your heart must be so filled with the Lord, there simply isn't any room left in there for questions you can't answer.

You don't know everything, Tyler once reminded me. And now I know that in spite of her music and the power of the Lord . . . neither does Grandma.

13

COLLISION AT RUSH HOUR

May

I ride home from school alone on my bike today. But when you ride home from school, you're never alone. You're always surrounded by a hundred other kids, racing to get home. Rush-hour traffic.

Kids at school are beginning to guess things are funny about my parents. Some kids even know what happened—or at least they *think* they know what happened. The newspapers barely said anything about it, but tragedies just have a way of making themselves known, even though nobody talks about them. Things just come out.

And people can be cruel.

The cruelness at my new school began with rumors. Nobody says them right to my face, of course, but I hear them all the same. The rumors go like this:

"I hear Preston Scott's mom was gonna marry Warren Sharp, and his dad shot her and tried to shoot Preston."

or

"Hey, I hear Preston Scott's dad shot Preston's mom right in front of Preston's eyes!"

or

"Preston Scott's dad is a psycho killer!"

I hear the lies and pretend I don't. I can handle them. I know that now. I'm older, and what happened—well, that's over. It's been more than a year since Mom died; Dad's trial has been over for months. I can just let stupid people's stupid words roll off their stupid tongues and then off my back like it was nothing.

I'm calm. I'm in control.

People who spread rumors, says Jason, *are wastes of life. They're like the people who read the* National Enquirer. *They've got such boring lives, they have to make up stuff about other people to get their kicks.*

As I ride home today, Jimmy Sanders—a kid in my English class—accidentally rams me on his bike.

"Oops," he says. "Watch where you're going, Scott."

He's only kidding—we both know that.

"Oh yeah?" I pick up speed and ram him.

"Ooh!" he says, laughing. "You *die*, Scott!"

He chases after me, but my legs are strong from football and track. I race up the bridge that crosses over the railroad tracks, leaving Jimmy far behind. I wonder if Jimmy is one of the people who's been spreading rumors. It wouldn't bother me if he is; I'm calm and under control.

People who spread rumors, says Jason, *probably have parents who believe Elvis is still alive.*

Jimmy catches up to me on the other side of the bridge. He rams me in our annoying little game of bumper tag.

"You're *slow*, Scott," he says. "That bike's a piece of *crap!*"

He speeds past me, and I change gears, pedaling hard in a high-speed pursuit. Nobody calls me slow. Nobody calls my bike crap. I rocket past a group of kids—a couple of them are girls I'd really like to go out with, now that I've broken up with Angela.

Angela and I weren't really right for each other. She talked a lot and complained that I didn't talk much at all, which isn't true; I talked all the time, just not to her. So we broke up, and it doesn't bother me. I'm never going to let breaking up with a girl bother me, I've decided.

Angela never knew about my parents. Actually, though, I think she did but just didn't say anything, and I never asked her.

"That's Preston Scott," says one of the girls we pass, and they start whispering secretly to each other as I speed out of view. I wonder what it is they're whispering. Are they saying good things about me? Do they like the way I look? The way I run? The way I play ball? Or are they whispering about other things?

People who spread rumors, Jason says, *like lies better than they like the truth. Don't trust anyone who spreads rumors.*

The girls disappear behind me as my bike speeds toward Jimmy. I don't care what the girls talk about. It doesn't bother me at all if it's rumors they're spreading. I'm better about that now that the trial's over.

I come up on Jimmy, ready to nail his tire, but he turns his wheel unexpectedly. I broadside him, our wheels lock, and we both eat it. I fly into a prickly hedge, and Jimmy lands hard on the asphalt. Our bikes clatter into a fireplug and stop. This is not fun anymore, and now I realize that it never really was.

Other kids stop to watch, figuring a fight is on its way. But they're wrong. They don't know me; they only think they do.

"You're an *asshole*, Scott," says Jimmy, meaning it with every fiber of his angry, bruised body.

"You didn't have to turn your wheel like that, moron," I say. "It was your fault."

Jimmy gets up and brushes dirt from his scraped knees. I ease my way out of the bushes.

"Like *hell* it was my fault," says Jimmy. "You can't ride a bike for your *life!*"

"Yeah?" I say, "Well, you have your brains up your butt!" Some of the other kids laugh.

Jimmy turns to pry his bike from the fireplug but then turns back with the last word.

"Maybe so," he says with his hands dangling by his side like a gunfighter waiting for the draw, "but at least *my* dad didn't kill my mom."

My ears hear it, and my brain gets it a moment later.

I can take that. It doesn't bother me at all.

And yet I'm all over Jimmy like a pit bull.

He can say what he wants. Everything's better now.

My feet, my hands, have a mind of their own. A sound comes out of my mouth like an Indian war cry.

I'm okay. I'm okay.

Jimmy puts up his fists, but his fists are useless. I grab him with my hands and throw him to the ground. I dive on him, growling like an animal.

It doesn't bother me. I can just walk away. I've said it over and over again until I can hear my head ringing.

People like that, Jason always says, *don't deserve the time it takes to punch them out.*

But here around me are my friends and classmates. They all heard it. And if they didn't know before, they know now—and my hands don't listen to me when I tell them to stop.

I smash Jimmy Sanders's head into the concrete again and again until I can hear his skull ringing. *It's over. It's been over for a year.* But if it's over, then why am I screaming? If it's over, then why can't I stop? Why can't I stop?

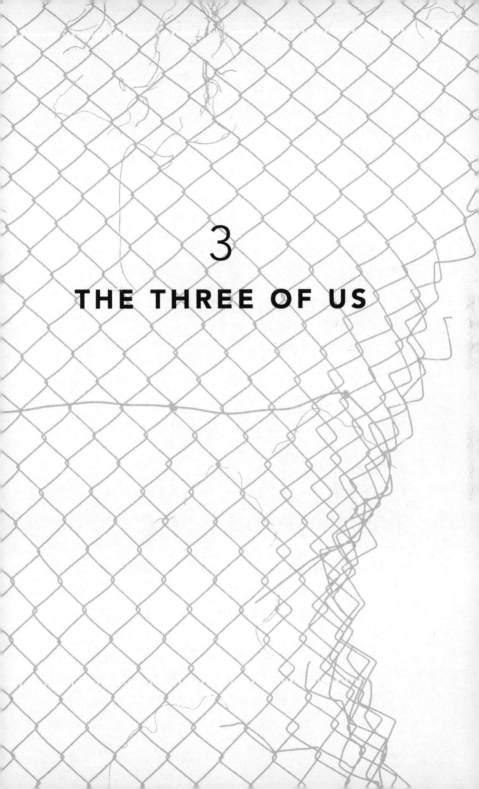

3

THE THREE OF US

14

THE LION AND THE LAMB

September—Eighteen Months After

"Do your knees hurt?" asks Dr. Parker, my pediatrician. "Do you ever get pains in your legs?"

I shake my head no, figuring if there's anything wrong with my yearly checkup, I won't be able to stay in football.

"Hmm," she says. "You've grown four inches since I last saw you. I thought you might have some growing pains. Guess not."

I suppose I have grown a lot. It's not just my size either—it seems everything changes when you grow. Suddenly your bicycle seat is as high as it can go, and you can reach the shelf above the refrigerator, and you can't fit into your old bed.

And memories change, too. They get flattened out and stacked up like pizza boxes. If I reach in, I can pull out any memory I want—Mom, Dad, *Family Feud*. But in some strange way, the memories are pressed down into pictures of a life that I can barely recognize. They seem like scenes from someone else's life.

Everything about me is changing. The doctor can see that. I'm no longer the little kid Mom used to bring in to see her with the flu or strep throat. I'm no longer that same frightened kid who had to hold Grandma's hand on the witness stand a year and a half ago.

"How old are you now, Preston?" asks Dr. Parker. "Fourteen?"

"Almost," I tell her. Fourteen'll be a good age to be, I think. It will be a good time in my life to be fourteen, now that things are calm, stable, and normal.

She puts her icy stethoscope on my chest and tells me to breathe.

"Still in football and swimming?" she asks.

"Football and track," I correct her. "A high-school coach told me that I'm almost ready for varsity in both sports, and I'm only in eighth grade!"

The doctor is impressed, but then catches sight of something and gently touches the skin around my eye, where she finds the last fading remnants of a black eye.

"How'd you get that?" she asks. "Football practice?"

"Naah," I tell her. "It was a fight."

She looks up at me with a troubled expression, then gets her penlight and points it into my eye, telling me to look at the wall. She stares right into my eye, and for a moment, I get the feeling that she's looking clear into my brain to see what makes me tick.

"You get into a lot of fights?" she asks.

"No, not really," I tell her. "Well, yeah, sort of," I finally admit. "It's because I've got this competitive nature. I get angry really easily—but I only let loose when it's a good time to, you know? I'll beat the heck out of kids who pick on my friends. I'll nail kids who cheat or lie or steal. I don't start fights," I tell her. "I just finish them—and I never pick on kids. I just defend them. I'm kind of like the school policeman."

The doctor smiles and shakes her head the same way my principal does.

It's not up to you to administer justice, the principal always tells me. But I always tell him right back that if it's not up to me, then who is it up to?

The doctor finishes looking in my eyes and gives me that concerned look again. It's like I'm back on the witness stand being questioned by the district attorney and I'm feeling guilty for telling the truth.

"It's not like I'm a bully," I tell her. "I'm real sensitive, too—I mean I cry and stuff."

She nods, but I'm not sure if she believes me. I *do* cry. I cry on Mom's birthday, all day. I cry on Thursdays in March. I cry on Christmas and New Year's and the Fourth of July and on any holiday that reminds me of her.

"I cry about as much as I fight," I tell Dr. Parker, "so it all balances out."

I think about how Grandpa Wes puts it—he has his own way of saying how I balance out. He calls me The Lion and The Lamb.

I guess I could be a lion. I sort of have this mane of blond hair. I guess I could also be a lamb on account of the tight curls of light hair that have been springing up all over my arms and legs. What Grandpa really means, though, is my mood swings. It's funny how I go from one extreme to the other so quickly. My dad's like that, too, only worse. Sometimes I think about how much my dad and I are alike. And it troubles me. The doctor looks at my growth chart, then up at me, then at my chart again, but I don't think she's thinking about my height and weight.

"Ever been in therapy, Preston?" she asks. "Have you ever seen a counselor?" No matter how casual and offhand a tone she tries to use, the question comes out sounding calculated. Dr. Parker knew my mom. She knows what happened to her. In the times I've seen Dr. Parker since then, this is the first time she's come even close to bringing it up.

"Yeah," I tell her, "I had therapy once." I have to think hard to even remember it. It was sometime before my dad's trial. This psychologist saw Tyler and me once and couldn't find a single thing wrong with us.

"That was it?" asks Dr. Parker. "Just once?"

"Yeah," I tell her, "he said I had less mental problems than most kids my age."

She chuckles, closes my chart, then reaches in her pocket out of habit to hand me a lollipop, but thinks better of it. Then she looks at my eyes one more time—not like a doctor, but more like that psychologist had.

"So do I check out okay?" I ask her. "Is there anything the matter with me?"

"No, Preston," she says, almost disappointed, "you're fine. I can't find a single thing wrong with you."

On Sunday I go to church with Grandma, Grandpa, and Tyler, like I always do. We pray and thank God for this miracle he's made in our lives. The miracle that we're okay—that we didn't lose our minds. That Tyler and I didn't turn into bad kids who hate themselves and everything around them.

For the miracle that Dad will be coming home.

I grip my book of hymns a little hard as I think about that. And although my voice sings about walking in the garden with Jesus, I think about walking through the prison with Dad.

He spent a year in jail before his trial, a year of his sentence was suspended, and they took over a year off for good behavior. That left him a prison term of a little less than two years, and it's just about up. Two years. A pretty good deal for a guy who killed someone.

The prison he's in now is so low-security that there are

barely any fences—and without fences he's free enough to dream. He has all these wild plans that seem to race out of all the prison gates with nothing to hold them back.

"When I get out," he says, "I'm gonna buy you that dirt bike I promised you."

"When I get out, we're gonna go white-water rafting, just the three of us."

"When I get out we're gonna drive cross-country. We're gonna see the Grand Canyon. We're gonna go sailing and skiing and camping. We'll go to next year's Super Bowl."

My dad likes to dream. I don't know where he'll get the money to do it all, but he promises, and I believe him. His last promise was that he and Mom would get back together. He broke that promise in a big way. Now he owes me, and he knows it.

After we sing hymns and hear announcements, the offering box is passed around. I drop a respectable amount of last week's allowance into the box. Grandpa says I really don't have to, but it couldn't hurt.

I wonder if Dad's in his prison chapel, thanking God for miracles, too. He got awful godly there in prison. He seems to be right up there with Grandma and Grandpa now.

"You people," my friend Jason says, "are like on a planet all your own with God—you talk about him so much."

And when he says that, I simply tell him the truth. "You have to trust somebody," I tell him. Trusting my parents didn't do me much good, and my old friends deserted me when Mom died. But trusting in God seems to have worked so far.

But Tyler, of course, still doesn't quite get it, and in the middle of a hymn about the Lord's heavenly throne and the firmament of His power, Tyler asks the Question of the Week.

"Exactly where is God?" he asks. "Exactly where is heaven? How far away?"

I nudge him, but he asks again. "Where is heaven?"

"How the heck should I know?" I tell him. "Do I look like God?" In the Bible they always talk about people rending their garments and gnashing their teeth. That's how I feel when Tyler asks me these questions. I nudge him really hard, and he bumps into Grandpa. Grandpa gently puts his large hand on Tyler's mop head, like the comforting hand of the Almighty, and it keeps him quiet until we're both dismissed to our Sunday-school groups.

"But where *is* heaven?"

Tyler spends half of his nights sleeping in the lower bunk of my bunk bed rather than in his own room. Usually I don't mind. Usually he stops asking dumb questions if I yell at him enough or pound his arm—but he's not letting up this time.

"Tyler," I complain, "it's school tomorrow. Go to sleep, huh?"

But my clueless brother will not hear reason. "Are you closer to heaven than me because you're up high?" he asks. "Are you?"

I try to ignore him by focusing all of my attention on the ceiling, which is lit dimly by Tyler's Donald Duck night-light. He's almost nine, and he still needs that night-light. He'll always be Grandma's little boy.

I try to find interesting patterns in the textured ceiling, but all I find are trapezoids and rhombuses and a bunch of other things that I just know will be on tomorrow's math test. I rub my eyes, but the shapes are still there.

"Are you closer to heaven because you're up there?" demands Tyler, as if his life depended on the answer.

I sigh. "Maybe. I don't know."

"Is it closer than the moon?"

"No," I tell him, but then I stop and think about his question. And my answer. "Yes. Yes it is."

"Good," says Tyler, and with his question finally answered, he promptly falls asleep.

But I am left awake. My eyes are open wide, three feet above him. Closer to heaven? I don't know.

"Stupid questions!" I mumble to myself, but yet I can see why Tyler needs answers. How can such dumb questions have such important answers? Such *hard* answers?

I know that heaven is farther away than the farthest star, and yet it's just as close as the night breeze against my skin. Mom's that way, too.

I won't sleep much tonight now that I've started thinking about Mom, and I'm half mad at Tyler, but half glad he's here, too, because the comforting sound of his easy, inno-cent breathing will keep me company. When I'm alone, I get caught up thinking about all the little things that could have been different and all the different lives I could have been living if, on that terrible Thursday, Mom had left the room, or sneezed, or turned around in time. Millions of different lives that I'm never going to lead. She'd be thirty-four now. Maybe she would have gotten back together with Dad in time, like Russ Talbert's parents did. Now no one will ever know.

The patterns on the ceiling are changing now. I can make out faces, but I don't want to see who it might be, so I close my eyes and think about Mom in heaven.

How close am I to her, really? I know the answer. I'm really just a breath away. Just a heartbeat. And the thought scares me so much that I thank God that Tyler's Donald Duck night-light is here to fight the shadows.

It scares me because sometimes I think about how close heaven really is, and how easy it would be to go there and be with Mom if I really wanted to. And sometimes I want to.

15

NIGHT ON THE FAULT

November

As I step out into the night, I can smell the aroma of dying fires coming from the neighborhood chimneys. It smells like Christmas. Judging by store displays, Christmas has already arrived. But since we're still eating leftover Thanksgiving turkey, I know it hasn't yet. Christmas is still a month away.

Dad's probably thinking about Christmas now. I think of him, sitting there in his minimum-security cell. I wonder if he's counting down the days until he's free, etching marks into the wall like prisoners always seem to do.

"Shh!" says Jason, even though I don't make a noise. Gently he slides his back door closed. It's a cold, still night. Cold for California anyway. There's a low-hanging mist, and dew on the grass that seeps through my sneakers, making my feet cold as I cross the lawn. A few more degrees and it could be frost.

It's three in the morning as we sneak out of Jason's house. His father sleeps like a log, and we'll be back before he even knows we're gone.

The homes on the street are all dark as we tiptoe off, afraid that the faintest noise could give us away. The night is so still, you can hear the freeway two miles away, like a fast-flowing river. Where are people driving to at three in the morning anyway?

By bike the trip to the railroad tracks takes only ten minutes, but there was no way we were going to risk opening the garage to get our bikes. By foot it's a half-hour trip.

"Do you think they'll be there?" asks Jason. "Or do you think they'll chicken out?"

"They'd better be there," I tell him. "I didn't get my butt out of bed the night before the biggest game of the year just to get stood up!" Then I shake my head. "Heather and her crazy ideas." Only Heather has the guts to suggest a picnic at three in the morning by the railroad tracks.

"Wait a second," says Jason. "Something must be wrong—weren't you dating Heather *last* week?"

I whack him on the top of his head, and it makes a slapping sound that echoes in the still night. He just laughs.

Jason, who must make lists and keep statistics in his sleep, has a list of all the girlfriends I've had. He can recite them in order like the presidents of the United States, and he does it just to annoy me.

"I swear," he says, "you go through girlfriends about as fast as you go through cans of hair mousse."

He, on the other hand, has been going with Colleen since June.

"What do you think we'll do once we get there?" asks Jason slyly.

"What do you think?" I ask him back.

"I don't know," he says. "The night is full of possibilities!"

"Not for you, maggot mouth," I say.

Jason shakes his head. "Nope. No maggots today. I brushed my teeth."

We both laugh, and then we shush each other, realizing that our voices can be heard for blocks.

Actually, we're not planning to do anything we really shouldn't, but anything you do secretly at three in the morning has the same excitement as if you really were doing something wrong.

We reach my street and steer clear of it, cutting across the park. As far as Grandma and Grandpa know, I'm staying over at Jason's tonight. They'd probably have a heart attack or something if they knew I was out. Grandma gets upset when I miss my ten-o'clock curfew. I shudder to think what she'd say if she saw me now!

Grandma doesn't think I like girls yet. She thinks I go out with them because they like me and it's what all my friends do.

But I like girls, all right. Sometimes I like 'em too much,

and I have to run a few fast laps around the park so I can stop liking them for a while.

The cold November night turns our breath into steam as we walk along. I rub my hands together to keep them warm. We walk quickly and get to the tracks before three-thirty.

We climb over the sound wall, using the footholds that were forged by unknown kids a generation ago.

The single track runs straight in both directions, south, all the way down to San Diego, and north up to San Francisco—maybe even farther. When I was really little, I actually used to believe that this was where the San Andreas fault was and that if we ever had "The Big One," this is where the quake would hit. The western half of California would break off on the dotted line of the tracks and sink angrily into the Pacific.

I look toward the greenbelt that lines the other side of the tracks, where we planned to meet Heather and Colleen. The strip of no-man's-land seems otherworldly: glowing tracks lined by the endless row of towering eucalyptus that were planted to break the wind when this was all farmland.

As I jump down from the wall and into the dark ribbon of land, I wonder how many other kids have snuck here in the middle of the night. These tracks run through the town where Mom and Dad met, twenty miles north. I wonder if they ever secretly met by the side of the tracks. Could it be that Dad gave Mom her first kiss in a secret place like this?

The thought drifts idly around my brain, but I shoo it

away. I will not get to thinking of Mom or Dad now. This is *my* time, not theirs. I won't let sad thoughts ruin it.

"I don't see them," says Jason. "Let's get out of here before we become train meat."

Far to the left, on the other side of the tracks, a flashlight seems to signal to us.

"Who's that?" says Heather, in the distance. "Preston, is that you?"

"Police," I say. "What are you girls doing here?"

A moment of silence, and then Heather says, "Shut up. You scared me."

"We thought you weren't coming," says Colleen. As we get closer, we can see in the dim moonlight that they've set up a tablecloth on the wet grass, and on it sits a basket filled with sandwiches and a six-pack of Pepsi.

Some other kids would be drinking beer, getting drunk and making idiots of themselves. But we're not other kids.

I sit down and put my arm around Heather, while Jason slides next to Colleen. We sit there for a while.

So we're here. Now what?

"Have a sandwich," says Heather.

"What kind you got?" I ask.

"Turkey," she says. "They're all turkey. We had lots of turkey in our house."

Even though I have turkey coming out of my ears, I take one and tell her how good it is.

We get to talking. We talk about teachers, and what our parents would do if they knew we were out, and what creeps the kids in math class are. Somewhere along the way Colleen, who's always bragging about something, brags about how her brother is a local motocross champion.

That's when Jason screws up royally.

It's bad enough when people put their foot in their own mouth.

But Jason manages to put his foot in *my* mouth.

"Preston," he says, "maybe you'd be good at motocross, too." Then he turns to the girls. "When his dad gets out next month, he's gonna buy Preston a dirt bike."

Heather's pretty quick. Sometimes too quick.

"Out from where?" she asks.

"*Back,*" says Jason, covering up. "*Back.* When he gets *back.*"

Jason must have thought that I'd told Heather—because he and Colleen tell each other everything, but I'm not like that. Heather's new in school, and all she knows about me is that I play football, which is all any girl needs to know about me. If I date a girl who doesn't know about my parents, I'm not going to tell her. Sure, I can talk about it now, but not to girlfriends. Girlfriends are different.

"Where's your dad coming back from?" asks Heather again. Colleen doesn't say anything. She knows about my mom and swore she wouldn't tell anyone. It seems as if she's kept her promise, but if we don't cover up quick, it won't matter.

"He's out of the country," I tell her quickly.

"He goes out of the country a lot," adds Jason.

"He's a pilot," I tell her.

Heather tilts her head and looks at my eyes funny, like Dr. Parker and the district attorney. She shines the flashlight in my face, so I'm blinded.

"I thought you told me he managed a supermarket."

By now Jason drops out and lets me fly this monstrosity alone.

"He does . . . ," I say. "I mean he used to."

"Oh," says Heather. "It's funny . . . but somebody told me that your father was in jail."

My fists clench in the dark by my side, but I quickly make the fists go away.

Even here, in no-man's-land, at almost four in the morning, my whole life still has to come down to the same thing: what my dad did. Why is that?

"He is," I tell her. I sigh, and tell her the whole story. What choice do I have now? But I make it quick, and I tell it to her without any feeling at all in my voice, so she won't get all choked up and pathetic about it. But she does anyway.

"Gosh," says Heather. "I'm sorry!"

"Don't be sorry," I warn her. "It's not your fault."

Now that I've told her, no one feels like saying much, so

instead we kiss for a while. Only now I'm not really in the mood to kiss anyone.

In the distance a train's headlight appears, just a pinpoint in the darkness. I hear a distant whistle, but the train seems to take forever to get any closer. We kiss a good five minutes before we can hear the churn of the wheels and the clang of the gate as it closes off the nearest avenue.

"Want to dodge it?" suggests Jason. It's just a joke, but I think I just might do it. I'm feeling angry, and there are no bullies to take care of. I'm the fastest runner in school. I could compete with a stupid Amtrak train.

Sensing that I'm about to stand, Heather digs her well-grown nails into my forearm to keep me from moving. Or maybe it's just because she's afraid of the approaching train.

The headlight grows. The whistle sounds, ten times louder than it was the last time. The moving light makes the dark shadows of the eucalyptus trees march along the sound wall like an army. The ground shakes as if there's an earth-quake and we're all going to be torn off at the dotted line.

But the headlight passes, and the train's three cars are gone in a fraction of a second.

"Who takes a train at four in the morning anyway?" I mutter.

"Maybe it's ghosts," says Heather with a smile, but even as she says it, her smile fades and she shrinks away from me.

"Sorry," she says.

. . .

The next day, after my football game, Jason and I sit on his porch throwing Christmas lights into the street to watch them explode.

"You know," he says, "I think Heather really likes you."

I shrug. "So? I like her, too."

"No, I mean she really likes you. Colleen told me at the game today that she thinks Heather is in love with you."

I grab a red bulb and toss it in the air. As it hits the pavement, it explodes like a miniature grenade.

"She's not in love with me," I inform Jason. "It's just that now that she knows, she feels sorry for me."

Jason hurls a green one at a pigeon pecking gravel in the middle of the road. The bulb explodes just next to the pigeon, and the pigeon takes off in a flurry of feathers, figuring it's been shot.

"I think she's even better looking than your other girlfriends," Jason says. "Colleen says you're the first boyfriend she's really had."

I take a blue bulb and squeeze it in my palm. "I've been thinking about breaking up with Heather," I tell Jason.

"Why?"

"I don't know. I just feel like it."

Jason gives me a disgusted look. "What's the matter?" he asks. "Run out of hair mousse again?"

The bulb in my hand shatters, but the tiny pieces of thin

glass are too fine to cut my skin. "I don't need girlfriends feeling sorry for me." I open up my hands and drop the tiny fragments. They tinkle on the ground. "I don't like her all that much anyway," I say, trying to convince myself. "And there are lots of other girls in school I can go out with."

"I think you're nuts," says Jason.

"Maybe so," I tell him, "but it's my life."

I don't need Heather's sympathy anyway. I got four touchdowns today.

16

SILENT NIGHT

Saturday, December 20

I'm locked in the closet again, and I'm mad!

This nightmare ended such a long time ago, it has no right to come back again. No right!

"I'm coming, Preston." I can hear Mom's voice, but I don't think it's really her voice. I can't remember exactly what her voice sounds like. I touch the doorknob. It's hot. My hand slips off it. A hot wind blows through the crack underneath the door and rises, tickling the hair on my leg.

I turn. The shirtsleeves around me try to smother me, they try to strangle me. But they're not sleeves after all.

They're ropes.

Wrapping around me, cutting into my skin, twisting around my neck like a noose. I reach the back wall, hoping to escape into my secret room, but it's a different closet. It's *the old closet in our old house. Small and dark.*

I kick at the door in anger, but it doesn't give. It's nailed shut.

"I'm coming, Preston," says Mom, farther away now. "I'm coming." It's all she ever says in this dream. Maybe it's a recording. I take a step back, and step on the vacuum cleaner. The ropes turn back into sleeves and fall to the floor as the vacuum comes on. I turn to look at it, startled. It's moving toward me. But it's not a vacuum cleaner anymore.

It's an engine.

A big hot grinding engine with groaning belts and sharp steel gears. The gears pull the shirts and coats into it, eating them with a sinister mechanical burp. The gears seem to smile. As the gears take in the edge of my shirt, I turn and smash my body against the door. The door is burning on the other side. I can hear it. The house is on fire.

But this closet isn't in the house, is it? I know that. This closet is in another place. It's in hell.

I sit up in bed, keeping the scream deep inside. No one must hear it. Not Tyler, not Grandma and Grandpa, nobody.

I calmly get up and change out of my sweaty pajamas into a clean pair. I open the door to my closet and step in. There is no vacuum. The shirts are just shirts. I push on the back wall and step into my secret room. Nothing scary in there.

Think of good things, I tell myself. Happy things. That will make me feel better. That will help me get back to sleep.

And so I think of Dad.

Where is he now? It's one in the morning. He's probably still in the car.

At 12:01, he stepped out of the prison. Wasn't a friend picking him up? He was going to take Dad to his parents' house. They're probably still on the road.

I step out of my room in my bare feet. The hallway is cold. Tyler's door is open a crack, and I can hear his steady breathing. No nightmares there. He still has little-boy dreams, even now. Even tonight.

Downstairs I rummage through the refrigerator for food, then sit in the den, eating junky snack cakes that I know will give me zits.

Across from me, next to Grandma's organ, is the Christmas tree—a six-foot Douglas fir, freshly cut and still green. But its arms are bare. They've been bare since we got it three days ago. Dad's going to help us decorate it this year.

Ah! Now I remember what Dad's doing now. He told us. He's gone to World Famous Tommy's to get a chili-burger. Sure—World Famous Tommy's is open all night, and where else do you go when you get out of prison?

I wonder if Dad will sleep tonight. I wonder what he'll do when he finally gets to his parents' house.

He'll probably just take a long hot shower.

He'll probably sit in a comfortable chair in his father's bathrobe and watch the sun rise on the first day of his freedom, while I sit here in front of our bare Christmas tree and wait for him.

Is he thinking of me now? Is he thinking about what we'll do when he arrives? Is he making plans?

When does the camping trip start? When do we go rafting? Is he making plans as we speak?

Or are you thinking of Mom, Dad? Are you calling to her in heaven, endlessly apologizing for what you did, and apologizing that you've been set free? Are you praying that the district attorney was wrong, and that she's happy for you? Are you praying that she forgives you for what you did and for surviving and that she gives you permission to start all over?

You're free now, Dad. You'll be home in a little while.

So why am I afraid to go to sleep?

17

CHRISTMAS PORTRAIT

In the living room, above the grand piano, is the big family portrait of Uncle Steve, Aunt Jackie, and, of course, Mom. My eyes always seem drawn to it, but today the feeling is worse. I can't help staring at it for most of the morning and half the afternoon, as I wait for Dad's three-o'clock arrival.

In the kitchen, Grandma waits for pies to cook, sitting as erect at the kitchen table as she does at the piano. She looks a little tired, a little concerned, and the fact that there's nothing in front of her—no newspaper or cup of coffee to give her attention to—makes me uncomfortable. She's just sitting there.

"It's a good thing that Dad's finally coming home," I say to her, just to see what she says back.

"Yes, it is, Preston," is her answer, plain and simple. The

tone of her voice is unreadable. She smiles at me, but the smile is unreadable, too.

In the living room, I am drawn to the portrait again. Mom's eyes look down on me. They follow me as I cross the room—portraits do that. Her eyes will follow Dad when he crosses the room as well.

I wonder how heavy the painting is. I wonder if we could take it down. Just for today.

I ask Grandpa about it.

"Don't be silly, Preston," Grandpa says. "Your father's seen that picture a thousand times before."

But then Grandpa looks at the picture pensively, suddenly not so certain of how silly I am. He goes over to it, and, putting his hands on either side, he tests the weight of the heavy frame. He stands back and looks at it some more.

"No," he says. "We can't start doing things like that. We can't start hiding all of Megan's pictures."

"Who's hiding all of Megan's pictures?" Grandma enters on the tail end of the conversation, figuring someone—probably me—is up to no good.

"It's just that Dad hasn't seen a picture of Mom in almost three years."

Now it's Grandma's turn to stare at the portrait pensively.

"Why don't you go play with your brother, Preston?" says Grandpa. "Sitting around will just make the wait even longer."

I leave the room. As I steal a piece of pie from the kitchen,

I hear Grandpa say, "Danny can't hide from her face all of his life, Lorraine. I won't help him do that."

Tyler isn't playing. He sits out front counting cars going by. "Thirty-two so far," he says. "I bet Dad will be here before a hundred." I sit next to him on the step.

"What do you think he'll be wearing?" asks Tyler. This is one of the more stupid questions he's asked.

"A dress," I answer.

Tyler laughs, and together we wait the hour until Dad's scheduled arrival.

Dad appears ten minutes early. The eighty-third car. It's Grandpa Scott's old Buick that Dad drives. Funny, but I was expecting Dad to drive his own car. I forgot that his car got sold even before he went on trial.

I feel some tears bubbling up inside, so I try to make them go away, but I can't. Dad doesn't pull into the driveway—he parks across the street, then crosses to us. I can already see that he is crying, too. He was crying before he even got out of the car.

He grabs both Tyler and me in an enormous three-way hug.

"You were waiting outside for me," he whispers through his tears as he hugs us. "I thought I wouldn't be able to find the place, but . . . I never thought you'd be waiting outside for me."

And for a short moment, right in the middle of that hug, it seems like nothing else matters. It seems like the rest of the stuff just didn't happen. But Dad can't keep hugging us forever.

We hang the ornaments on the tree one by one. Dad looks at some of the fancier ones as we do. *He's looking at the ones from our old tree,* I realize, but I don't want to mention it to him. He sees that I notice, and he self-consciously hangs an ornament on the tree.

Tyler and Grandma string popcorn and cranberries on thread. "It's good to have you here, Danny," she says.

She and Grandpa hugged him and cried, too, when he stepped into the house.

He must have felt like he had crossed into the Twilight Zone when he stepped over that threshold. He has never been here, and yet he must recognize it. His old furniture is in here, mixed in among Grandma and Grandpa's, the way weird fragments of your life mix in your head at night, making those dreams that are too bizarre to remember. This whole house must be so familiar to him and at the same time so new.

When the tree is finished Grandpa plugs in the lights, and we all stand back to admire the sight of the colored bulbs casting a rainbow of pine shadows across the walls. But Dad's not looking there. He's looking off toward the living room, where Mom's eyes scrutinize him from the wall.

• • •

Dad takes Tyler and me shopping at the mall. Actually, we take him. He has no clothes to wear but the ones on his back, so his father gave him some money to buy new ones.

In the crowded pre-Christmas department stores, we wait outside the fitting rooms to give him thumbs-up or thumbs-down on his wardrobe selections.

He takes us out for pizza and eats it slowly, like a man savoring a gourmet meal.

"I almost forgot what good pizza tastes like," he says. We talk about the usual stuff. School, the end of my football season, and the beginning of the track season. Tyler's mean third-grade teacher. It's all stuff he already knows, but we talk about it anyway. Besides this stuff, we don't say too much to each other over dinner. I keep my mouth full of pizza to cover those tense silent moments with chewing.

As I look at him, I begin to see him the way he must have seen our living room—very familiar, but also strange and new. Almost frightening. He's been gone so long, it's as if I don't know who he is anymore. Maybe that's why on his first day of freedom, we've already run out of things to say.

He stays late this first night. We sit in front of the tree, watching a boring Christmas special. Tyler falls asleep in his arms, and Grandpa lets Dad carry Tyler off to bed. I have to remind him which bedroom is Tyler's.

"You can visit the boys whenever you want, Danny," says

Grandpa after Tyler is snug in his bed. "Just let us know when you want to come over."

Before Dad leaves, he comes into my room just as I'm getting ready for bed. I can't believe he's really finally free—yet having him here doesn't feel as good now as it did when he first hugged us at the door.

"I guess you're way too big to be tucked in," he says.

"Naah," I say, then slip under the covers. "Tuck away."

He comes over to my bed, thinks about it, but doesn't do it. He smiles at me. "No. I think maybe you *are* too old."

And then he just stands there.

He must be thinking the same thing I am. *What now?* We'd been waiting so long for him to get out. Now that he is out, what happens next?

He stands there for a moment, then says good night, but I don't want him to go. Not like this. When he got here and he hugged us on the porch he wasn't a stranger. But it seems like he'll be leaving as one.

It's funny—when you're little, you accept your parents for what they are: your parents. And you never give it a second thought. I really never knew anything about Mom until after she died and Grandma and Grandpa started talking about all the things she had done as a girl. Until then, she was just Mom. Dad was just Dad.

But Dad's not just plain Dad anymore.

He can't be, because just-plain-Dads don't do what he

did. And as I sit here on my bed, I realize that I don't really know who he is. Besides the fact that he's my father, I hardly know anything about him. That never seemed important before or even while he was in prison. But now it is.

"What are you thinking about?" he asks me.

"I'm just wondering what *you're* thinking about," I tell him.

"Well," he says, "I'm thinking about how last time I saw you in this bed, you took up half of it. Now your feet just about hang off the end!"

I look at my feet. I can't remember when they didn't reach the end of the bed. Dad reaches over and turns out the light. In a moment he'll be out the door.

"Can I ask you a question, Dad?"

"Sure," he says.

But what can I ask him? I want to ask him all about all the things that ever happened to him—everything he ever felt and thought and did, 'cause maybe then I could understand *why*.

But where do you begin to ask that? And how could I ever lead up to asking that final question. *Why?*

I think I know where to begin. It's a question I always wanted to ask when I was younger—something I always knew was not to be discussed, so we never discussed it. Ever.

"Dad," I ask, "how old were you when your sister . . . you know . . . drowned?"

Dad casually grabs onto my bedpost, as if the question has shaken him but he's trying hard not to show it.

"I was really young, Preston," he says. "I was nine."

I take a deep breath and force out the words. "Tell me what happened."

Dad doesn't say anything. I can hear him breathing, but my eyes haven't adjusted to the dark. I can't see him yet.

"Why do you want to know about that?" he asks in a near whisper.

"Because I do," I tell him. "I want to know what happened."

My eyes start to adjust, and I can see the edge of his hair lit by moonlight, but his face is dark, like an eclipse.

"You might have nightmares," he warns me. "I'll tell you some other time."

"No . . . I'll be fine." I already have nightmares. What's one more?

Dad sighs and waits, hoping that I'll say "never mind." I almost do, but I keep my mouth shut.

"It was a big family reunion," he begins. "My parents and my sister and I all drove out to Arkansas where I was born. I hadn't been there since I was five though, so I didn't remember it much.

"Anyway, we camped out about a mile away from a big river, and one of my aunts decided it might be nice to have a picnic down by the riverside. She took me, my sister, and my cousins down there for a picnic lunch."

I listen, and I try to imagine Dad being nine—as old as

Tyler is now. I can't picture it; all I can see is Tyler. He says, "We brought a bunch of inner tubes that were all pumped up, so we could sort of float down the river—I mean the river wasn't wild or anything, there weren't any rapids, so we figured it would be all right.

"So all of us kids get out our inner tubes after lunch, and my sister and I are the first to start floating downstream. That's when my tube starts to leak."

"*Your* tube?" I ask.

Dad nods.

"But you could swim, right?"

"No, I couldn't swim a stroke yet. So the air was leaking out of my tube fast, and the water we were drifting down to was getting rougher and deeper. I started to get scared.

"Well, my aunt and cousins, who were still onshore, saw what was happening. I was losing air, and my sister, who couldn't swim either, was floating farther and farther away. They all decided that, since they couldn't swim well enough to come out and save us, they would grab onto a tree on the shore, and take hands, making a human rope. They would stretch themselves out to us."

"Did it work?"

"No. The water was rougher than it looked, and their feet started to sink into the mud at the bottom. They couldn't do it. And they went under one by one.

"I remember my father telling me how he and my uncle

could hear us all screaming a mile away. It sounded like the end of the world, he said, as they got in the car and drove over the hill. They were screaming themselves because they knew something terrible had happened.

"Anyway, I don't know how, but the water sort of pushed me to shore. And I lay there half alive until someone pumped the water out of my lungs."

Dad doesn't say anything more. It's as if he's sitting there watching himself on the shore, almost lifeless, waiting for someone to save him.

"And your sister drowned?" I ask.

Dad looks up at me suddenly as if there were something I had missed.

"They all drowned, Preston," my father tells me. "All of them."

And in the silence that follows, I can hear that one scream of the aunt I'll never meet multiplied five times. "No!"

"My aunt, my sister, my cousins . . ."

This is too much to know. Too much to hear all at once. All of them. Nobody told me that. Why doesn't anybody ever tell me things? Now I know why Dad's father had a nervous breakdown. Has this been on my father's mind since before I was born? Every time he falls into a deep depression, every time he just sits there not talking to anyone, just staring out lost in his own thoughts? Is this what he's thinking about? Was he reliving the awful day his family died trying to save him? How could anyone live with that weight? How could anyone not lose their mind?

"It's not your fault," I tell him. But it doesn't matter what I say. I can see his eyes reflecting the dim light. I can't tell if he's crying, but I can see what he's feeling. He blames himself. He's always blamed himself.

"Of course it's not my fault," he says quietly. "It just happened." But even as he says it, I know he's still trying to convince himself. *If it weren't for me*, he's thinking, *they'd all still be alive.* I can almost hear it playing over and over in his mind, the same way I play that horrible night Mom died over in my mind. Stuff like that gets trapped in your head and just bounces back and forth and can't find a way out. *I should have died*, he's telling himself. *I should have died, too, Preston, and if I had, then the other things would not have happened.*

"It's okay, Dad," I want to tell him. "Terrible things happen to good people for no reason that we can figure out." I want to tell him I understand, *because it happened to me.* I wasn't much older than you had been, Dad, when the awful thing happened to me, too.

But my lips won't move. I can't say a word.

I could ask him about Mom now. This would be the time. I could ask why he did it—what he was really thinking when he got the gun. What on God's earth could be so hard to bear that the only way to end the pain was to shut down his mind, go crazy, and take my mother's life?

If I asked him now, he would tell me, he wouldn't lie, I know that. And if he told me, I would understand—like I understood about his sister and his cousins and his aunt. I know that, too.

The words are on the edge of my lips, and my heart pounds knowing that I could finally, after three years, ask my father what has become the most important question in the world. I could ask him now.

But I don't have the guts.

I slip under my covers, ashamed that I can't speak. He stands up, thinking that I'm shrinking away from him, but then he leans forward and gives me an awkward hug. Somehow it's like we're back in the awful gray jail and the glass is still between us, and even as he hugs me, I feel like he's hugging me through glass.

He straightens himself up, turns, and slowly walks to the door.

I can't ask him about Mom, can I? I never *will* be able to do it, will I?

"Dad," I say as he leaves the room, "I love you." But the door closes behind him before he can hear.

18

THE QUESTION OF THE WEEK

January

Three weeks later Dad moves in with us.

"But I couldn't move in with you," Dad protests when Grandma and Grandpa make their offer over Sunday dinner.

"Nonsense," says Grandma. "You're here visiting the boys almost every day; we have the extra room. There's no reason why you shouldn't—it solves everyone's problems."

"Maybe the boys could move in with me and my parents instead," suggests Dad. Sometimes I feel like I don't have any say in it.

"And change schools in the middle of the year?" says Grandpa. "No. We're perfectly content to have you stay with us until you can get yourself an apartment nearby."

Dad has a job now. A friend of his got him the job—the same friend who picked him up at the prison. So now Dad's a manager at a paper company. But he still can't afford his own apartment. At least not one in *this* neighborhood.

"I just wouldn't feel right," says Dad, "just moving in on you."

"Well, if you want to be with the boys, there's not much of a choice, Danny," says my grandpa, "because the boys are staying with us—whether you move in or not."

And I begin to wonder what will happen when Dad does get his own apartment. What will Tyler and I be expected to do—where will we be expected to go? And I wonder if I'll have to take sides again, like I used to when Mom was alive.

On the first night that Dad stays with us, I hear a noise from his room. It's very soft and very muffled, but I still hear it.

Dad is crying. He's crying the way I cry sometimes when I think about Mom. All alone in my room, I can bury it in my pillow so no one will come in and ask me what's wrong. That way I can keep it all to myself, and nobody can make me stop crying until I feel good and ready to. Maybe that's what Dad's doing, and maybe I should just let him alone. But I can't just sit here and listen to Dad cry.

I tiptoe out of my room and cross the hall to his. Grandma and Grandpa don't hear him; they're still downstairs watching TV—I can see the shifting blue light from the television hitting the banister, casting long shadows against the wall. They don't hear Dad. Tyler is asleep. It's only me.

Without knocking I open the door a crack and peer in.

Dad is sitting on his bed, his head in his hands. He's sniffling and quietly sobbing. He doesn't know I'm watching him.

I wonder if he is crying about Mom. I wonder if he cried about Mom after it happened. He cried about Tyler and me. He cried about what he had done, but did he ever cry about Mom? I didn't see him for months after it happened so I have no way of knowing . . . unless I ask him, and I'm not about to do that.

I open the door wider, and it creaks, giving me away, so I step in.

"You okay, Dad?" I ask.

"I'm fine, Preston," he says, trying to put an end to his tears. "I'm just feeling kind of funny, that's all."

"About what?"

Dad doesn't quite answer that. Maybe he doesn't know how to put it into words. He just sits there a bit longer, not saying anything.

"I don't deserve all this," he finally says. "I don't know why I'm being given it; I don't deserve it."

I figure he's talking about Grandma and Grandpa letting him live here, but somehow it goes beyond that, doesn't it? He doesn't deserve to be free. He doesn't deserve the fact that we still love him—that we can all turn away from what he did and forgive him. But Grandma has a good way of putting it. She says, "If the Lord can forgive mankind for killing His son, then surely we can forgive the man who killed our daughter." The hard part is accepting it.

"Everyone's too good to me," says Dad, drying his eyes. I go over to him and he gives me an awkward hug. I don't feel anywhere near as emotional as Dad does now, and I feel a bit weird about how he's acting. I can't see what the big deal is.

"I made an oath when I was in prison, you know," he says. "I swore that when I got out—and if you still wanted me—I would spend my life making sure that I was the best dad I could ever be. I'm going to take you places, I'll buy you whatever you want. I know things can't be the way they used to be, but . . ."

"But they're going to be better," I say.

He smiles and hugs me tightly, and no matter how old I am, when my dad hugs me, I can believe anything's possible.

But Tyler still doesn't quite get it.

And sometimes it makes me mad.

Not long after Dad moves in with us, we get a call from Tyler's teacher. I'm at track practice, so I don't know a thing about it until I get home. By then, things are in a sorry state. Grandpa's pacing back and forth in the living room. Grandma's gone off to speak with Tyler's teacher, and Tyler is in his room with the door closed.

The only bit of good luck about this situation is that Dad isn't home from work yet.

I ask Grandpa what happened, but all Grandpa says is, "Maybe you ought to talk to him. Your grandma and I talked to him, but I don't know if we're getting through."

I know what they mean. Tyler is still Smiling Tyler. Even when he's not smiling he has this kind of glazed look in his eyes, and you don't know whether he's listening to you or thinking about yesterday's sports scores.

I go into his room. Tyler is lying on his bed, calmly throwing a ball into the air and catching it.

"You get into trouble at school?" I ask him. "You cheat on a test or something?"

"I just asked a question," he says, never breaking the rhythm of the game of catch he's having with himself.

"What did you ask?"

"Just a question."

"What kind of question makes Grandma have to run off to speak with your teacher?"

"Beats me," says Tyler. "It was just a question."

The ball goes up; the ball comes down. I'm losing my patience. "Why don't you tell me what you asked?"

"It was just a question," he says, "that's all." He hurls the ball harder. It hits the ceiling and comes back down hard against his chest. He grabs it and smashes it against the ceiling again.

I take the ball away from him, feeling my temper, which always hangs by a thread, begin to fray.

"Do I have to punch you out to get you to talk?"

"*It was just a question!*" he screams, already in tears at the thought of being punched out. He's such a basket case sometimes. "Just leave me alone."

Tyler rolls over and sobs, with no sign of stopping. I'll get nothing out of him, so I go ask Grandpa again.

Grandpa, who is still wandering aimlessly in the kitchen, seems not to want to tell me either, but finally he gives in.

"He asked his teacher," says Grandpa, "if it's all right to kill someone."

Just hearing the words, and knowing the fact that Tyler asked them, makes me furious, and afraid. What did he mean by asking that?

"Now they'll probably want him to go into therapy," says Grandpa.

"He doesn't need therapy," I tell him. "He needs to be straightened out." And I head back off into his room to do just that.

"Preston!" says Grandpa, concerned that I might hurt him or something.

"I'm just gonna talk to him," I tell Grandpa as I push my way back into Tyler's room.

Tyler is still sobbing on the bed, rolled halfway into a ball, facing the wall.

"*It was just a question,*" says Tyler, between his sobs. I grab him, sit him up, and shake him.

"Where the heck do you get off asking a question like that?" But doing this only makes him sob harder, so I stop shaking him, and hold him firm. I know what I want to say to him. Maybe it's not what Grandpa wants to say, but it's what I want to say. And if Grandpa were one of Danny Scott's sons, he would understand.

"Tyler," I say, "look at me. Stop crying and look at me now!" Tyler listens. He holds down his sobs; his face fades from scarlet to pink.

"You are never to ask anything like that ever again to anyone, do you understand me? Do you understand?"

"Yes," he mutters.

"You don't talk about Mom, and you don't talk about death, to your teachers or to Dad or to anyone. And what happened to Mom, now that Dad's back, you have to pretend like it never happened."

"But it did happen."

"*I don't care!*" I tell him. "You pretend like it didn't. You want to think about Mom, fine. You think about her when you're in your room. You cry by yourself, but you never let Dad see it. And any other time, you do like I do; you push it way, way down inside you until you can't feel it anymore. You be a man."

He's crying harder again; yet through his tears, I hear him whisper, "I miss her."

I loosen my grip on Tyler's arms, and I slip my hands around his back, hugging him tightly. He needs this hug. He needs this hug like I needed Grandma's hand on the witness stand. "I do too, Tyler," I whisper back.

"But I won't tell anyone," he says. "I won't tell."

19

INTERFERENCE

March—Three Years After

Tyler and I are a team in no time at all. We learn all the ins and outs of life with Dad as quickly as we can: the knowledge of things to talk about and not talk about, the art of steering conversations away from certain topics. We run interference for my dad, because he needs protection. I know this. He needs protection from people and things around him.

We protect Dad from the television.

A news show comes on one night while Dad and I are stretched out on the couch in the den—a grisly story about a man who axed his family. Nothing like Dad, but still it's about murder, and it's about a family. If Dad sees it, he'll think about what happened to Mom—but the problem is I can't just change the channel, because if I change it, he'll know why I did, and that would be just as bad as him seeing it. I look at the TV guide. There's nothing much else to watch, so changing the channel now would be a really suspicious thing to do.

I casually get up and find Tyler in the kitchen, trying without luck to spoon out some rock-hard ice cream that has been in the back of our freezer.

"You need help with math now," I tell him quietly.

"Okay," he says. He leaves the ice cream to thaw and goes up to Dad in the den. "Dad, I need help with my math," he says. Dad is so eager to be of help that he jumps up and follows Tyler into his room.

"Math is easy, Tyler," says Dad. "It's just a matter of patience." Tyler finds his workbook and turns to a page in a unit they probably haven't even started on in school. He keeps Dad away from the TV for at least half an hour.

We protect Dad from kids at school.

Dad picks me up after track practice one day. I can see him waiting by the edge of the field watching me finish up my last few laps. I think about my friends. Jason likes my dad— the three of us always play basketball in my driveway.

"If they let him out of prison," Jason once told me, "then they must have had a good reason to, so it doesn't bother me." Most of my friends think that way. But not everyone in school is my friend—and as I look around, I can see that all the other sports are letting out at the same time. Some of these kids know, or might figure out, that this man is my father. I know some kids who would keep their distance and yell nasty things at him and snicker—like they used to do to me.

So I leave practice straight from the field, without changing in the locker room.

"You should shower, Preston," Dad says.

"Showers are broken," I tell him. "I'll shower at home."

"How about your books?"

"No homework."

We get into the car and get away from that school as quickly as we can.

We protect Dad from women in church—the single or divorced women who see Dad as an attractive man all alone with two boys and think he's "available." He needs protection from them, too—no doubt about that. Dad's polite when he talks to them, but we make sure it ends there. He knows Tyler and I never want another mom.

He's not available. Period.

At one church gathering, a woman with skinny legs and hair that's too short slithers through the crowd toward my father. I spot her coming a mile away. Dad stands nearby, alone and vulnerable.

Next to me Grandma talks with one of her friends who is complaining about back pains. Thinking quickly I turn to Grandma's friend and say, "My dad knows exercises that would be good for your back."

Dad turns to me and chuckles. "I do?"

"Sure," I say. "You lift weights, right? You know all about exercises and stuff."

Dad seems baffled, but Grandma's friend looks toward him for some serious advice, so he fakes his way through it.

Meanwhile the skinny-legged woman lingers on the sidelines, patiently sipping a Coke, waiting to pounce as soon as Dad stops talking.

I "accidentally" brush past her, and her Coke spills all over her too-skinny dress.

"Excuse me," I say, then turn back to see her heading toward the ladies' room and away from Dad.

We protect Dad from family get-togethers—and that's the hardest interference play to run.

On Easter Sunday, Tyler and I conspire to play a game called "Where's Uncle Steve?" It's a game I think we'll have to play for a very, very long time.

The game goes like this: the whole family comes over to Grandma and Grandpa's. We must know where Dad is at all times. We make sure that no one is talking about Mom in any room that my dad might enter. We make sure our younger cousins—who don't know any better—don't say anything stupid.

And we keep Dad away from Uncle Steve any way we can—because I know that if Uncle Steve and my dad as much as looked each other in the eye, there'd be a nuclear explosion that would obliterate our entire town, lake and all.

"*You took him into your home?*" I remember Uncle Steve screaming when he heard about Dad moving in with us. Uncle Steve never screams. He's the quietest guy I know. "You took that killer into your home and let him live with you—eat your food?"

Grandma and Grandpa both had to talk him down. This is the same man Dad used to take fishing when Uncle Steve was "Piggy Poodle" and only ten years old. Dad was like a big brother to him. But none of that seems to matter anymore.

"How can I forgive him?" yells Uncle Steve. "He stole my sister from me—your daughter. And how did he pay? He spends a couple of years in jail, and now he's out, and life's wonderful? Is that it? Everything can be the way it was before—is that what he thinks? *Well, it can't be.* He has no right to think it will be, and you have no business trying to make it like it never happened."

I have nightmares when I think of what might happen if Uncle Steve actually ever spoke to my dad.

For the first part of the long Easter afternoon, Uncle Steve sits in the living room, making conversation, so I challenge Dad to a game of one-on-one on our driveway basketball court. When Uncle Steve comes out front to have a look at Aunt Jackie's new car, Tyler lures Dad into the backyard to watch him do flips off the diving board. When it's time for dinner, and Dad may actually have to pass the potatoes to Uncle Steve, I insist on eating at the big table—because I know there's not enough room.

"Daddy, can you eat with us?" asks Tyler, clinging onto Dad's arm and pointing at the kitchen table that is reserved for all the kids, and the problem is solved. Dad agrees, and eats in a different room from Uncle Steve.

It's after dinner, during the final quarter of our "game," that Tyler and I begin to get sloppy. We are full of food, and we're lulled into a false sense of security as we listen to Aunt Jackie and her rich fiancé, Gary, talk about how well Jackie's interior-decorating business is doing and how, when they get married, he's going to build her a dream house that she can design and decorate. They talk about their dreams together, and I get all caught up in it because I think it's the same fantasy Mom always had—a successful business of her own and a husband who loves her but is also rich. If Mom were still here, she and Aunt Jackie might have gone into business together, and then they would have finally gotten over their little jealousies. It was silly, but Mom always thought that Aunt Jackie was more successful than her, and Aunt Jackie always thought that Mom was prettier.

Then I suddenly come back to earth and realize that no one is keeping track of Dad and Uncle Steve.

It is now that Tyler and I realize that they didn't need us to play the game for them—they play it fine all by themselves. When my dad walks into a room, Uncle Steve stops the conversation and walks out.

Then when Uncle Steve walks into a room, Dad disappears, silently dissolving into the woodwork.

Uncle Steve looks at Dad only once during the whole day—almost by accident, on his way out the door with his family. Dad happens to step into the foyer as they're leaving, and Grandma takes his hand, as if to reassure him he's still part of the family. That's all fine and good, but now Dad's stuck there in the same room as Uncle Steve. Uncle Steve says good-bye to everyone, except my father. Instead he throws my father a gaze that's both burning hot and icy cold at the same time. Then he looks at Grandpa once and turns to follow his wife and kids out the door.

I know what he was thinking when he looked at Grandpa— it's the same thing he was thinking the last time he was over.

"It's an awful thing you're doing, taking him in like this," he told Grandma and Grandpa. "It's awful."

Once he is gone and the door is closed, I breathe a sigh of relief.

I can't stay in that house after Easter dinner; I have to get out and away from all the bad feelings. I hurry down the street, my walk becoming a jog, and my jog becoming a sprint. I can feel dinner bouncing up and down in my stomach as I run. I get to my school as fast as I would have if I had been on my bike. And once I'm there I begin circling the track, trying to purge my mind of Dad and Uncle Steve.

It's an awful thing you're doing.

My lungs feel as if they're going to burst, but I push harder, and harder. There are no hurdles out on the track, so I imagine them. I start to leap the imaginary hurdles, but all I can see are the hurdles falling as my foot bangs into them.

Your daughter is rolling over in her grave.

I leap higher and higher, but in my mind the hurdles continue to fall.

Life would be so much easier without people telling us what we're supposed to feel—what we're supposed to do. Life would be so much easier if everyone left us alone.

But now I *am* completely alone. There is nothing but the track, and that's the way I like it. And I keep bounding over the hurdles until I clear them and they stop falling down.

20

DAD'S LOBOTOMY

March—Four Years After

The gunshot rings in my ears.

I explode from the starting blocks with controlled fury. I hold nothing back. Just because I am the favorite to win doesn't mean I can't be taken.

Nothing but the track. Forget the cheering crowds; forget everything but the hurdle looming up in front of me.

The runners—who all began staggered twenty feet ahead of each other to make up for yards lost or gained in the turns—are closing in behind me as I close in on the ones in front of me.

I throw my right leg out and leap. The hurdle sails beneath me and rocks slightly with the wind of my passage. My foot makes contact with the ground once more. I pound through the dirt to the next hurdle and fly above that one as well, and the next, and the next.

Now we are in the straightaway. I am neck and neck with the star hurdler from the other team. It's him or me.

So far today I've won both the 200-meter and 400-meter sprints. I won't lose this one.

I turn on my second stage and blast in front of him, leaving him far enough behind so that I can't even hear the pounding of his feet. Only my own.

I cross the finish line but don't slow down even though I know I've already won.

Grandpa Wes, who has been my private coach and trainer this year, is already on the field to congratulate me.

"Fine run, Preston," he says, patting me on my sweaty back.

"Thirty-nine point two seconds—that's your best time this season."

I shake my head. "Not good enough. It should be down to thirty-nine flat by now."

"Don't be so hard on yourself," he says. "You're only fifteen—you've got time."

"You're my coach, Grandpa—you're supposed to *push* me," I tell him.

He laughs. "Preston, you're the fastest hurdler on the team and you're only a freshman. What more do you want?"

I smile at him. "The hundred-meter dash."

• • •

When the meet is over, the magic fades from the field, just as it does after a football game. The cheers of the crowd are replaced by thinning murmurs as everyone leaves. My stubborn single-mindedness is replaced with all those thoughts and feelings I can get away from when I'm running. Like the fourth anniversary of Mom's death less than a month away. Thursdays in March hang over me each year like the blackest of clouds. That day never seems to get any farther away or any less painful.

My teammates' families filter onto the field. Mothers hug their sons, and my teammates, feeling too old for that, squirm out of the embraces. They don't know what they have.

I, on the other hand, have my grandma and grandpa, my dad, and my little brother. It's wonderful to have that, but still I'd rather be like my friends and have a mother. I don't think I'd take her for granted.

Grandma grabs me tightly and kisses me, smearing lipstick on my cheek. "Oh, we're *so* proud of you, Preston," she tells me, like she always does. Dad hugs me next, and Jason, who is still the most loyal friend in the world, stands back, waiting for the affection to end. Jason's grown quickly and is taller than me now, but I'm much more solid.

Grandma takes my one second-place and two first-place ribbons from the day and puts them in her purse for safe-keeping. "You've got so many of these, I don't know where you're going to put them."

"Maybe you can give them to me," says Tyler. I tell him that he'll have his own one day, but it's not much consolation. Tyler just smiles, like he always does, and quietly accepts it. Maybe I will give him one.

As we walk off the field, Grandpa turns to me and asks, "Where will you be sleeping tonight?"

Dad answers before I do. "At home," he says.

"Oh," says Grandpa, "at *your* place, then."

I suppose Dad's place is home, but I sort of have two homes. I'm not sure which one is my *real* home.

The apartment Dad, Tyler, and I moved into last summer wasn't home at all—it was too small, and we all spend most of our time at Grandma and Grandpa's anyway—after all, they were just down the street.

Then Dad bought a townhouse a little farther away. That was my real home for a while, until Grandma and Grandpa bought the townhouse right next door.

It's funny, but it seems Dad just can't put any distance at all between him and my grandparents. Not that he'd ever want to.

My room in Dad's house is just on the other side of the wall from my room in Grandma and Grandpa's house. Jason jokes that I can bang on the wall if I hear myself playing my music too loud.

"Get to bed early tonight, Preston," says Grandpa as he and Grandma leave. "If you want faster times, you need a full night's sleep." Then he turns to my dad. "You make sure of that, Danny," he says. Dad nods, taking his orders cordially.

Dad's very good about doing what he's expected to do. He works long days and comes home to spend all his evenings and weekends with Tyler and me. He's a model father and very "morally upstanding," as Grandma would say. He had better be, because he knows that if he weren't, Grandma and Grandpa might take Tyler and me away from him. Although no one ever talks about it, we all know that Grandma and Grandpa are still our legal guardians. We only live with Dad because they give us permission to.

On the way off the field, I pat Dad on the back, preparing to head off with Jason. "We're going to get pizza," I tell him. Dad is not pleased.

"What about the barbecue?" he asks. "What about the movies, Preston?"

It had completely slipped my mind that Dad had planned a little family night—his famous barbecued ribs and a trip to the Cineplex—just the three of us.

"Naah," I tell him. "I think I'll just have pizza."

Dad is disappointed, but he just lets it go. "Maybe we'll all go get pizza," he suggests.

"Naah," I say. "You can barbecue. Save some for me."

Dad is disappointed again, but still he just lets it go. He turns without the smallest fight and heads toward the car with Tyler. "See you tonight," he says.

I think for a moment, then say something I know I really shouldn't. "I'll probably be home late," I tell him.

He turns, and for a moment I think he's going to shake his head and impose a reasonable curfew on me, but instead he just deflates. "I'll leave the porch light on," he says, then gets into the car.

Even though I've gotten exactly what I asked for, I feel lousy and I wish I were back on the track running again.

"I don't see the problem," says Jason. "Your dad's a nice guy, he gets along with your friends—he lets you do what you want."

"Yeah, but that's part of the problem," I tell Jason over pizza—but he can't quite understand. He didn't know my father before. First of all, Dad used to be much, much stricter. I guess it's good that he lets me make my own decisions—I mean, I'm old enough now where I should be able to—but I'm amazed at the things he lets me get away with. Breaking curfew without explanation—not calling when I don't come home for dinner. I mean, I know when I do things wrong, and although I won't tell him, there are times when I know I should get in trouble for it—but Dad just pretends he doesn't see or pretends it doesn't matter. Even on the rare occasions when he does punish me, the punishments are so wimpy they don't mean a thing. It's almost as if he's afraid of me. I don't know what there is to be afraid of.

"Sometimes I break rules on purpose just to get him riled—just to get him mad enough to get on my case," I tell Jason, "but he just doesn't."

"So? That's a problem?"

"Yes!" I say, frustrated over the fact that he just can't understand. "It's like he's had a lobotomy."

Jason takes me seriously. "Probably not," he says. "They don't do that sort of thing in prison unless you're really bad off."

I angrily fling a pepperoni at his face. It grazes his nose, leaving some tomato sauce rimming his nostril.

"Hey!" he says, throwing a piece of Canadian bacon at me. "What's the deal?"

"Just forget it," I tell him. "You're just cluelessly brain-dead." I toss my pizza onto my plate. I really don't feel like eating pizza anyway. I feel like eating barbecued ribs.

Annoyed, Jason pushes himself away from the table and stands, pointing an accusing finger at me. "This is *your* problem," he tells me, "not your father's. I wish my father was as cool as yours is."

"Get a clue," I tell him, fighting a losing battle to have the last word.

"Get a life!" he responds. But I already have one. And when I think about it, it seems the only person around here who doesn't have a life is my dad. I wish he did have one. Not one that I tell him to have and not one that Grandpa Wes and

Grandma Lorraine prescribe for him—but one of his own. Maybe if he did, this weird feeling would go away.

God nails me for wishing Dad had a life.

The punishment has a name. And her name is Sarah. She's this five-foot-four bundle of redheaded energy who moved into our neighborhood from Chicago and slithered close when I wasn't looking. She has three children of her own: a girl Tyler's age, a boy a few years younger, and a toddler of undetermined sex that never stops screaming. On the annoying scale, her children rank somewhere between mosquitoes and thermonuclear war.

I know Dad likes Sarah, but I try not to think about it. She's nice enough, but she has no business being around my dad. She ought to just leave him alone, but I know she won't and Dad probably won't leave her alone either.

While Tyler is out playing with his friends one afternoon, Dad calls me into the living room for a "talk." He never looks at me when we have these "talks." It's part of this lobotomy thing. Now he looks away, and looks down, and looks at his hands. He just can't look me in the eye.

"I just wanted to ask you if you knew someone," he says.

"Who?"

"Sarah Walker."

He must be blind if he thinks I don't know her. "Yeah, I know her."

"Well, I was thinking of maybe taking her to dinner."

"So?" I say.

"So I just wanted to know if it's all right."

Well, what does he want me to say to that? *Yeah, sure, go ahead. Go out with any woman you want. No problem; you're a bachelor now.* There are these demons in my brain, and they huddle together like linebackers, trying to tell me how I should run my defensive plays. They want me to tell my father no. *If you've got such power over him, tell him no, they say. If you're that threatening to him, if he's that afraid of what you'll think or say or do, then TELL HIM NO because we don't want him to ever look at another woman again. We want him to live like a monk for the rest of his life,* say the demons in the huddle.

"You can do whatever you like," I tell him. "You don't have to ask me."

"You won't be upset at all if I see her?" he asks, not quite believing how easy it was.

"No, it's no problem," I tell him.

He smiles. "You're quite a kid, Preston," he says before he goes to call Sarah for their first date.

Sure, I think, he can do that. He needs it. I don't mind. Just as long as he never gets married. Just as long as he never asks me to call another woman Mom.

21

THE PTERODACTYL

April

Sarah is pretty, intelligent, fun to be with . . .

And she doesn't know.

That is the state of affairs when we go out with her and her kids for a let's-get-acquainted dinner six weeks after Dad started dating her.

Maybe she's like some of my old girlfriends, I think—the ones who knew about Dad but pretended they didn't. Maybe she's waiting for Dad to tell her. Dad promises he will—he's just waiting for the right time. "She has a right to know," he says, but it must be pretty hard to work up the guts to tell her.

The demons huddling in my head secretly hope that when she knows, she'll run in the other direction and never look back. But otherwise I want my dad to be happy.

We eat at a fancy restaurant that I know Dad can't afford,

and the table is clearly divided by family lines—us blonds on one side of the table and Sarah with her redheaded kids on the other. I try not to talk too much during the meal, because I don't feel like it. Tyler's good at that—speaking only when he's spoken to. He can spend whole meals making patterns in his spaghetti or trying to spear peas one at a time. He's a natural at disappearing at a table full of people, but I'm not. I have to shovel food into my mouth constantly—otherwise I'll feel uncomfortable keeping quiet.

Davey and Dina, Sarah's two older kids, are dressed up like Tweedledum and Tweedledee in matching color-coordinated outfits. Mercifully she left the bawling toddler with a baby-sitter.

"Mommy, the chair is too hard," complains Dina.

"Mommy, can't we sit at the table by the window?" complains Davey.

I keep my mouth filled with breadsticks.

"You're such a good athlete, Preston," says Sarah, already on her third glass of wine. "I've seen you at the football games. Number thirty-two, right?"

"Preston's also a state champion in track," Dad brags. "He runs in invitational meets all across the country."

"Really!"

I shrug. "Seattle, San Francisco, Tucson," I say, my mouth filled with breadcrumbs.

"I hurt my leg once running," offers Davey.

"Sarah's athletic," says Dad. "She bowls. You oughta see her—she's very good."

"We all bowl," says Dina. "We're *all* very good."

Tyler tunes all this out. He spends the first part of the meal refolding his napkin in a variety of fascinating shapes, like squares and rectangles.

Dina drinks a whole pitcher of water before the salads arrive, then says she has to go to the bathroom, but returns quickly. "The bathroom's too disgusting," she announces. "I'll wait."

Throughout the meal, Dad acts like a used-car salesman, trying to sell us on Sarah and her kids, and trying to sell Sarah on Tyler and me. Actually, I don't mind Sarah, considering the circumstances. She seems nice enough—she's friendly and outgoing. But Dad is pushing way too hard, and I'm starting not to like it. And I definitely don't like the way Dad looks at her. He has the same smile—and the same warm eyes—he used to have when he looked at Mom. I can't stand it, and I have to look away.

Most of the conversation seems to revolve around Davey and Dina and what tragic situations they've had to endure, like the *tragedy* of divorce, and the *tragedy* of losing bowling competitions, and the *tragedy* of the chicken pox smack in the middle of Christmas vacation.

"It was the worst vacation of my life," announces Davey tragically.

When the conversation slips to our family, it is invariably some talk about me and sports—Tyler barely gets mentioned at all. But as always, Tyler seems not to mind. It's not my fault—it's just that other people seem to talk about me whether I want them to or not. And Tyler has learned to thrive in my shadow. He enjoys disappearing into his world of napkins and peas and spaghetti designs. Sometimes I wish I could.

"Mommy, my meat is too rare," complains Dina.

"Mommy, this chicken smells funny," complains Davey.

It is sometime during dessert when Dad mentions Sarah's singing.

"Oh, I only sing for fun," says Sarah with false modesty. "I'm not very good."

"I heard the demo you made. It's pretty good," I say.

And then Tyler suddenly emerges from behind his ice-cream sundae.

"I know someone who sings better," he says.

I reach my foot over to step on his to try to shut him up, but I miss.

Sarah keeps her eye on Tyler. "Who's that, Tyler?"

Dad appears almost as ready to wet his pants as Dina is.

"My grandma," says Tyler. "My Grandma Lorraine." Dad and I breathe a loud sigh of relief that almost comes out in perfect harmony. Relaxed again, we begin to talk about Grandma—her singing and her piano and organ, and all about how she found God when she was ten.

"When she plays the organ," says Dad, "it's so beautiful, she could charm the angels themselves."

Tyler emerges from behind his sundae once more.

"My mommy's an angel," says Tyler.

This time *I* almost wet my pants.

The uncomfortable silence is broken only by Davey sniffing the pudding on his plate.

"Of course she is," says Sarah, kindly and sweetly. "She's an angel in heaven. Your dad told me."

But Dad didn't tell her everything. I know that. I know by the way Dad looks away from her when she says it.

I look at Tyler in this uncomfortable moment, and only now do I realize what's really going on here. These little comments aren't coming out because Tyler's a bit out of it—Tyler knows exactly what he's doing. Smiling Tyler is controlling all of us. Even now there's that tiny Tyler smile on his face. The little devil! He couldn't do any better if he had voodoo dolls to stick pins in. I have to smile, too. I never gave him that much credit.

"So what do you think of Sarah?" Dad asks us the second we leave the restaurant.

"I don't like her hair," says Tyler from the backseat. "And she's too short." He thinks for a moment. "Other than that, she's okay."

"How about you, Preston?" Dad waits for me to answer. I take a moment too long just to make him sweat, but then I get mad at myself for being so nasty about it.

"Yeah, she's great," I say. "I mean, I don't know her very well, but she seems okay."

"So you like her?"

"Yeah, I like her."

"Do you like her a lot?"

"I like her," I say again. He's pushing it.

"At least she's pretty," mutters Tyler, as if that makes up for any problem in the world.

We drive home the long way and Dad keeps his eyes too attentively on the road, making believe the road is all he's thinking about. It's just like the way I concentrate on the food on my plate when I don't want to talk. Finally he says what's on his mind.

"I'm going to tell her about Mom this week. About the 'accident.'"

"Are you going to call it an 'accident'?" The words slip out of my mouth before my brain has a chance to censor them.

"I'm going to tell her the truth," says Dad, keeping his eyes on the road, but running a stop sign all the same.

"Good," I say, with my tongue now firmly harnessed. "She ought to know if you're going to keep on dating her." The word *dating* stumbles on my tongue. Dads don't date. The two words just don't go together.

"I have to tell her," says Dad, "because I think things might be getting serious between us."

Hold it! Hold it! Serious how? Serious as in *love*? Did *that* slip in behind my back when I wasn't looking? Dating and love are two completely separate things.

"Someday," says Dad, "I might want to ask her to marry me."

If I were driving, I would have stomped on the brakes and squealed to a halt in the middle of traffic. Unfortunately I won't be driving until next year. I turn away from my father so he doesn't see my eyeballs bulging. But he catches my reflection in the misdirected side mirror.

"I hope we get a bigger house," says Tyler.

"Preston?"

Inside my head, the demons have broken the huddle and are laying siege to my mind. How dare he just decide this. How long has he known her, two months or so? How long has he been out of prison, a little over a year? How long since he killed Mom?

But I deny any of these questions exist. I deny feeling anything. I am a disciplined athlete. I am in control of my body and mind. I feel nothing but happiness. That's what I tell myself.

"Preston?"

"When are we going white-water rafting?" I suddenly spit out at him like an accusation.

"What?"

"I'm happy for you and all that, Dad—you and Sarah;

that's great—but when are we going white-water rafting like you promised?"

I've caught him off guard. He stutters a bit.

"Well, Preston . . ."

"When do we go rafting and skiing and camping? When do we see the Grand Canyon? When do I get my dirt bike? When do we do all those things you promised?"

"We'll do all of them, Preston," he tells me. "We'll do them with Sarah."

"Fine," I say. "I was just asking."

Dad promised me the world when he was in prison. I don't want the world, I want my mom back, but he can't perform that particular miracle, can he? So if the world is all he can give me, then he better get on the job.

Because if I can't have the world, then he can't have Sarah.

Dad gives me a small slice of the world. He gives me the dirt bike he promised, against all my grandfather's protests, and we spend the day riding it up and down the street—Dad, Jason, and I. Its loud, rude engine draws the angry attention of the neighbors and the admiration of all the kids on the block.

The noise is enough to bring my grandfather out of his house.

"What is this?" he asks while Dad is off for his ride.

"It's mine," I tell him. "Dad got it for me."

His face turns to stone. I immediately sense this is going to be worse than I'd thought.

"I see," says Grandpa.

As soon as my dad gets back from his ride, Grandpa calls him aside. "Danny, can I speak with you?"

Jason takes off buzzing down the street. I lean one ear into Dad and Grandpa's conversation.

"Who gave you permission to buy him a dirt bike?"

"He's my son," says Dad. "Why do I need permission to buy him anything?"

"You know Lorraine and I don't approve of those things. They're dangerous. And we're still his legal guardians."

Dad steams whenever Grandpa reminds him that they still have legal custody of Tyler and me. It's a cold reminder that we're only with Dad because of their good nature. It's more than enough to make Dad back down.

"He'll only ride it when I'm around," Dad says. "On weekends. In empty parking lots—places where there's no traffic."

"You should take it back," says Grandpa. "Get him something else."

"No!" I say, busting into their conversation. "This is my dirt bike. Dad bought it for *me*. I'm not taking it back."

Grandpa looks at me, then at Dad.

"You see what you've done, Danny?" he says as he leaves. "You see what you've done?"

But nobody, not even Grandpa, is going to take this bike away from me. I've had enough taken away from me already, and it's about time I demanded something back.

• • •

Dad seems sullen for the rest of the day. He lets Jason and me ride the bike, but he won't ride it himself—he just sits on the porch and watches. When Jason leaves and we put the bike in the garage, Dad says what's on his mind.

"Maybe your grandpa's right," he says. "We should take it back." But he won't look me in the eye when he says it.

"Why are you afraid to stand up to him, Dad? You don't stand up to anyone anymore."

"What am I supposed to do, Preston? I feel like I'm still on probation. If I do something wrong they'll take you away from me."

"They love you, Dad," I remind him. "You know that!"

"But they love *you* more," says Dad. "Both you and Tyler. And they'll always wish you were in their home again. If they get mad enough at me," he says, "they'll take you away. I don't want to lose you, Preston."

"I live where I want to live!" I tell him. "It's *my* choice, and I want to live with you. Even if you marry Sarah."

"I appreciate that, Preston, but the bike . . ."

"The bike stays!" I say, and I stare my father down. Finally he leaves the garage, and I'm left alone with the bike.

I've won the battle, but I don't feel good about it. I tried to make my father stand up against Grandpa, but that's not what happened. Instead, not only did he back down from Grandpa, I made him back down from me as well.

Next time, I say to myself, I'm going to back down first. Next time I will. I'll sacrifice some of my own pride and self-respect, and give Dad back some of his.

Dad has Sarah over for dinner almost every night, or we go over there. I once asked Grandma how she felt about them getting so serious so quickly. She always answers such questions the way Christ himself might.

"Danny's had a very hard life," says Grandma. "He deserves a second chance. And as for Sarah, we'll just love her, too. We'll love her like she were our own daughter."

But Sarah's not their own daughter. Not even close. . . . Her relationship with Dad is not what I would call perfect. It's not an equal sort of thing—it's mostly just Sarah pushing and pulling Dad in every direction she can. She drags him to a party one day, a show the next. She gets tickets to things and doesn't even tell my dad until she arrives at the door ready to go wherever it is she decided they must go. And the worse part of it is that sometimes she leaves her children with us.

When we had dinner that time with her, she seemed sweet enough. I didn't see that her fingers weren't fingers at all, but talons, and she was slowly digging them deep into my father's skin. "She's strong willed," says Dad. "What's wrong with that?" If it were just that she's strong willed, I'd like her just fine. But there's a difference between being strong willed and demanding complete control.

"She's a woman who knows what she wants," says Dad, "and knows how to get it."

Maybe that's why when they went to L.A. to see a show, Sarah came back wearing a necklace that we all know my dad can't afford.

Maybe that's why Dad's always over at her house fixing it up and redecorating it just the way she wants it.

"She's a very determined woman," says Dad.

I say she's a reptile.

"You'll all move in here when your father and I get married," she says as she gives us a tour of her house one day. "Preston will get his own room, and Tyler will get to share one with Davey—he'll like that. And we'll build a workout room with a whole gym in the garage. Who needs a three-car garage anyway? Two is enough for anybody."

We're all sort of just swept along in the enthusiastic beating of Sarah's slick reptilian wings. We're all hooked by her pterodactyl talons whether we like it or not.

Maybe this is what Dad needs, I try to convince myself. Someone to give him direction. Someone to keep his mind so full of details that he doesn't have to think about anything. But even as I think it, I realize that the last thing Dad needs is someone else telling him what he ought to do.

"I hate Davey," says Tyler one day when we're driving back from Sarah's place. This is new for Tyler. Tyler never admits to hating anybody. It's enough to make Dad prick up his ears about an inch.

"Well," says Dad, "he does whine quite a bit, doesn't he?"

"They all do," I add. "I think they're all just spoiled rotten."

"Life with Dad'll unspoil them," says Tyler. "'Cause Dad's so cheap."

I laugh, but I wonder just how cheap he will be. Sarah will have him spending his money left and right. Like . . .

Like Mom did.

Dad shakes his head. "Sometimes I don't know about those kids."

"You're not dating the kids; you're dating Sarah," I say. Dad accepts my reassurance.

"And you really like Sarah?" he asks, as he always asks. Do I like Sarah? I like her when she doesn't drink too much. I like her when someone else has to talk to her instead of me. Do I like her? Not really.

"I like her if you like her, Dad," I tell him. "I want you to be happy."

I don't tell him that I wish Sarah would crawl back under the rock she came from. I don't tell him that I wish something absolutely awful would happen to make Dad dump Sarah and those miserable larval lizards she calls children once and for all.

"I'm glad you like her, Preston," says Dad with a smile. "We're all going to be very happy."

"That's right," I say. Or at least we'll all pretend to be.

22

WHO DO YOU LOVE?

May

On a Saturday night, while my grandparents are away, I have a little party at their house—Jason, me, and a bunch of other friends.

I see less and less of my father lately—he's always doing odd jobs for Sarah. He's at her house today fixing something up or building a wall or putting up wallpaper. She monopolizes his time as if she owned his soul.

"She's not a woman, she's a career," Grandpa says.

But if Dad likes her, fine. Dad can do what he wants.

And so can I.

Downstairs, the music is blasting, and somebody mans the blender, making chocolate shakes. At least I think it's just chocolate shakes. I know some people brought beer, but it's not my job to tell them they shouldn't do it. I watch out for myself. It's not like *I'm* drinking or anything.

My friends dance in the living room and lie around on the sofa talking. The place gets a bit messy, but as long as I leave everything the way I found it, Grandma and Grandpa probably won't mind. They probably won't even know.

Before it even gets dark, my dad appears at the front door.

"What's going on here, Preston?" he asks.

"What does it look like?" I say, trying to look cool. "It's a party."

"Did Grandma and Grandpa give you permission to do this?"

"They're not here; they don't care," I say.

Dad looks around—kids with beer, loud music.

"No," says my dad. "No, I don't think so. This party stops here."

And for the first time in as long as I can remember, Dad looks me in the eye.

"You're coming home, now."

"No," I tell him. He's humiliating me in front of all my friends. Nobody does that. I don't care who he is.

Dad goes over and turns off the stereo. It's amazing how all that noise can just collapse in on itself with the flick of a switch, leaving a room full of people who don't know what to do.

"Everybody out," he says.

But everyone just lingers there. Like they all stood and

watched on the day I pounded Jimmy Sanders's head into the sidewalk.

"This isn't your house!" I yell at him.

"You're coming, Preston. If I have to drag you out by the roots of your hair, you're coming."

"Why don't you just go back to Sarah? Doesn't she need you to clean between her toes or something?"

Some friends begin to snicker. People start whispering. Gossiping. "That's Preston's dad," I can hear them say. "He's the one who . . . you know."

"Preston, say good-bye and we'll clean this mess up."

But I don't move. Not yet.

I should give in. I told myself I would. This doesn't matter, I tell myself, I can just let it go.

But my friends are here around me watching. And it's time to take sides again.

It's over, I tell myself. The party was over the second Dad walked in, so just give in, and walk away with my tail between my legs. *It's over.* But if it's over, then why am I so angry? If it's over, then why can't I stop yelling at him? Why can't I stop?

"Who do you think you are!" I scream at him.

"I'm your father!"

"Well, that doesn't seem to mean much anymore, does it?"

He is not going to take this party away from me. He's never going to take anything away from me ever again. If he can marry the flying lizard lady, then I can have this party.

Dad turns beet red in the face like Tyler does when he cries. Only Dad's not crying.

"You have no respect for me, do you?" Dad screams. *"Why don't you respect me? Why?"*

It almost makes me laugh. Why? Do I really have to tell him?

"Why do you think?" I growl, and then I explode out the back door and head for the garage.

My dirt bike flies through the Saturday twilight at a breakneck pace. I take turns at full speed, not caring if I fall. I rev the rude buzz-saw engine to annoy everyone in the neighborhood.

I can do what I want. For weeks I've had to ride this stupid thing in parking lots and closed-off streets with Dad supervising me. But I'm fifteen and can do what I want, and he's not going to stop me ever again.

I race through a red light. I don't care.

He thinks he can fall in love and be happy. Then why can't I be happy? Why? No matter what I do I still feel something is missing. Why is it that no matter how hard I push it down, Mom's face always comes back up? It's all I think about when I see Dad with Sarah. I can tell myself it's all right, but I'm lying. It's *not* all right.

And why can I still see his horrible hand on that awful gun?

I round the corner spinning past my old school, the junior

high, where I made friends and enemies. Where idiot kids spread rumors about things they didn't know.

It doesn't matter how busy I keep myself. How fast I run, how many passes I catch, how many friends I have. It doesn't matter because he still did it. I can't change that.

I ride over the railroad overpass and past the spot where Jimmy Sanders made me blow a gasket. I could have killed Jimmy, I think. If adults hadn't pulled me away, I could have killed him. I've got that in me, too, don't I? It's like my whole life comes down to my dad. It always has. It always will.

I hate Grandma and Grandpa for making me still love him. Uncle Steve is right. We're all crazy. We're all deluded. I should never have let him in my life again.

It's dark now. I turn into the long greenbelt that runs on either side of the railroad tracks, and I race along the grass, my bones acting like shock absorbers, until the bike flies out from under me and I crash to the hard earth.

God, what's wrong with me? I'm crying like a baby—I'm shaking.

I love my father. I do. I love him so much it kills me, but I hate him more than anything in the world. How can anyone feel both at the same time and still be in one piece?

I want to make him hurt as much as I do, but I want him to be happy.

I want him to suffer for the rest of his life, but I want him to be healed.

I want him to hold me, but I want him locked safely away in that burning closet of my dreams forever and ever.

Love and hate. Why can't those feelings just cancel each other out, so I feel nothing at all? That's what should happen.

A train whistle rattles my brain. The shadows of eucalyptus trees begin to march like an army. I begin to run, picking up speed, running alongside the tracks. I'm at my peak now. I'm the fastest I've ever been, fueled by all these awful feelings.

But the train.

It races past me like I'm standing still, and in a moment the marching shadows are gone, the train is gone, and I fall to the ground in exhaustion.

I'm just not fast enough to outrace it, and no matter how hard I try, no matter how much I push myself, I never will be.

When I get home, Grandma and Grandpa's house is dark, empty, and clean. Dad cleaned it all by himself. I can hear the TV over in Dad's house next door, and it takes all my courage to go over there and walk in.

Dad says nothing as I come in. I say nothing to him.

But as I turn to walk upstairs, I hear him talking calmly from the living room. In control of his emotions. In control of me.

"Taking the bike out like that was dangerous," he says. "You broke our agreement. Tomorrow I'm taking the bike back."

I don't turn to him. I don't dare to look at him now. I bite down and swallow my anger and my pride. "All right," I tell him, "take it back."

When Grandma and Grandpa come home the next day, I go and stay with them for a while. As always, they're understanding and glad to have me there. But being there doesn't feel right. Nothing I do feels right anymore.

"I could never figure out how it could be so easy for you," I tell Grandpa one morning while we're alone in the kitchen. "The way you could just forgive Dad like that, and get on with it." Sometimes I think they're absolute saints.

Grandpa lets out a halfhearted snort of a laugh. "Easy? You call this easy? Football practice is easy, Preston. Fighting a war is easy. But this?" Grandpa sips his bitter coffee and shakes his head. "Every morning I still have to wake up and remember that my little girl is gone because of Danny, and I have to remind myself that in spite of it we still love him, and I have to pray that I can keep on loving him. That's not easy, Preston. It never has been."

23

THE LAST OF SARAH

June

Dad decides not to ask Sarah to marry him just yet. "This is all happening too fast," he confides to us one day. "I need some time to think things through."

Smart move on Dad's part.

I speak to Jason almost every day to keep him informed of the latest developments. He's the only one I can talk to about this.

"Sarah's been acting awfully weird lately," I tell him over the phone, hoping it's not bugged. "She calls Dad seven or eight times a day at work to complain about the painters, or the fact that Dad hasn't finished building the gym in her garage, or some other stupid unreasonable thing."

"Go on," says Jason, "I'm listening." He laps it all up like it's a soap opera. Sometimes I feel like my life *is* just God's little afternoon drama—something to keep Him entertained when hanging clouds with Mom gets dull.

"She even calls him out of important meetings, because she thinks she's more important."

"No way!"

"She gets him in trouble at work, right? And then when he stops by her place in the evenings, she complains that he doesn't work hard enough for her. She drives him like a mule—worse than a mule, like a slave."

"Lose this woman," advises Jason. "Lose her in a big way."

I agree with him, but I don't think it's going to be easy.

At first Dad's plan was just to cool it with Sarah for a while— but after what she did when Dad talked to her about it, we all think it's a better plan to pull out entirely. She has us all really spooked.

"I knew she was high-strung," says Dad, "but she's worse than that. She's just plain crazy!"

She scares him. She scares all of us.

"When I said we needed a break from each other, she just went nuts," Dad tells us. "She started throwing things. Books, bottles." And then Dad looks down. "I was afraid she was going to kill me," he says. Sarah might be small, but when she's angry, she's powerful and frightening.

The last thing Sarah said to him was that he had better come back and take away the whole workshop of tools he had been using to fix up her place. Grandpa suggests that Dad go get his things when he knows she's not home.

"It'll make it easier on everyone," says Grandpa.

But Dad won't do alone. "I want a witness," says Dad, "because no matter what I take, she'll accuse me of stealing from her. And who are the police going to believe, an ex-convict or a woman with three children?"

So Grandpa goes with Dad, and they come back before dusk with some of the smaller stuff.

"Thank the Lord that's all over with," says Grandma once the truck is unloaded.

But it's not over with. In fact, as far as Sarah is concerned, it's only just beginning.

It's about midnight when we hear the first crash. We're all sleeping at Grandma and Grandpa's house because Sarah's been threatening all week to come over and do all sorts of things. We figure we're safer if we're all together in a different house.

The first crash is the window. It wakes me out of a sound sleep. I know right away that it's our place next door. Then more crashes. I hear things tearing, things thudding against the wall and hitting the ground in pieces.

"Dad!"

Dad is up, and I can hear him bounding down the stairs. Grandma and Grandpa awake from a deep sleep and don't know what to do. It's robbers, I think, robbers breaking into our place, looking for valuables to steal.

But it's not robbers, it's vandals. In fact, it's one single vandal.

I look out the window and see it sitting right there, halfway up the curb—Sarah's car.

"Call 911," cries Grandma.

"No," says Dad. "No police!" The last thing Dad wants is a run-in with the police now that he's off parole. He races outside and to our house next door to do battle with Sarah, who seems to be very drunk and very, very angry.

"I want my key!" I hear her scream to Dad. "I want my key back now. You broke into my home. I want my key now, or I'll call the police."

And somewhere deep down inside me there's a part of me that's resting very comfortably and satisfied while the rest of me sits on pins. The demons aren't huddling or waging war at the moment. Instead they're sitting in the jury box, passing judgment, and they tell me that this is just what I wanted to happen, that Dad is getting a taste of what he deserves.

And I sit upstairs listening to Sarah rave like a madwoman, I can't help but think that I was the one who wished this upon my father.

Round One ends. Sarah drives off, but Round Two begins even before Dad has a chance to tell us what happened.

Sarah returns in five minutes with reinforcements. Two huge, scuzzy-looking men with arms as wide as my head drive up behind her in a beat up black sports car. She must have picked them up at the 7-Eleven down the street.

Their fists are already curled, ready to do damage to my father. My God! What lies did Sarah tell them to get them here? What are these men going to do to my dad when they find him?

If it was up to Sarah, they'd . . .

. . . they'd kill him.

Their heavy fists bash against the front door. Grandma's hands tremble as she dials 911. But it will take too long for them to get here—we should have called before. Maybe we'll get lucky—maybe the neighbors called.

Dad stands back in the foyer, pacing and waiting. The door bulges in. The whole house shakes with each pound of the door.

"I want my key!" screams Sarah.

This is all too unreal. If it weren't so terribly awake, I'd think it was just another one of my awful nightmares.

Tyler stands safely at the top of the stairs, but Grandma stands downstairs, too close to the door. I grab her and force her back.

"They'll hurt you, Grandma," I say as I push her upstairs. "They want to hurt all of us. I don't want them to hurt you!"

Now the two men kick at the door. The sharp crashes

seem loud enough to crack the house in two. The lock won't hold much longer.

And then finally we hear sirens.

They approach from the left and the right. They are outside our house in an instant. I can see the blue and red lights chasing each other around the living room.

The kicking finally stops, and then everything is quiet for a moment. And then there comes the politest of rappings on the front door.

Two policemen pace around my grandparents' living room. The 7-Eleven thugs talk outside to a third officer, explaining their side of the story. The neighbors all stand outside and gawk, probably thinking that this murderer who moved in down the street just murdered someone else. Sarah sits in the kitchen, just beginning to calm down, and Dad sits in the dining room. Sarah's anger turns to tears, which she blots away as quickly as she can. "We were going to get married," she mumbles to a policeman. I begin to feel a bit bad for her.

"He has my key," she says. "He broke into my house—I want my key back!"

"Do you have her key?" the policeman asks Dad—as if this were all Dad's fault.

"Do you have Miss Walker's key?" the officer asks again. Dad doesn't answer. Is he going to lie to the police? I know what he's thinking—if he gives back Sarah's key then Sarah has won. Most of Dad's tools are still there. She has the gym equipment, which is ours. She'll never give it back to us.

"Do you have Miss Walker's key?" says the policeman, about ready to slap the cuffs on Dad for not answering.

Dad looks up at him. "Yes, I have it."

The policeman puts out his hand. "Then give it back."

In Dad's house it looks as though everything we own has been dropped out of an airplane. Our furniture is shredded and overturned. Pictures are broken—paintings taken off the wall and split over chairs. Clothes are torn and strewn everywhere. She went as far as to take food from our refrigerator and grind it with her furious hands all over our nice white carpet—and all this in a matter of a few minutes.

She even took my trophies and smashed them against the stone mantel.

Our whole lives are here, smashed about us on the floor. And Dad stands in the middle of it, looking around, helpless to really do anything about it other than collect the debris. Some of this stuff just can't be saved. We all know it.

"I don't have much luck with women," he says. There's nothing funny about it, but I smile feebly anyway. Next door Grandma and Grandpa put Tyler to bed and calm their own nerves. I'm glad they're not here now. I'm the one who should be cleaning up with Dad. We're in this together. We've been in this together ever since I first sided with him on the day he and Mom broke up.

"I've had this coming to me for a long time," says Dad. "Maybe Sarah is possessed by your mother," he says, only half joking, "and she's trying to pay me back for what I did to her."

I shake my head. "Mom wouldn't have done something like this," I tell him, "no matter how angry she was. She has more class."

Dad bends down and picks up the ruined sofa cushions, gently putting them back into place.

"It's better this way anyway," he says. "Even if none of this happened, I couldn't love Sarah the way she needs to be loved." I can see Dad's eyes getting moist. "How could I love Sarah when I still love your mom?"

A tear flows from his eye. He dries it quickly and hurries to busy himself with work. There's so much work to do. He stands up a broken lamp and carefully puts on its shade.

I go to pick up an armless, headless trophy. Looking at it, I can see it's only a cheap piece of plastic. I thought it would mean more to me, but it doesn't.

It's half past three in the morning now. At half past three, it's easier to ask those questions that never see the light of day.

"Dad," I ask, "why did you do it?" I swallow hard. "Why did you kill Mom?"

Dad puts down the lamp and sits on the floor. I don't know if he'll answer. Maybe he'll just go on cleaning.

He rubs his hand across his face a few times, and it makes a slight scratching sound on his beard stubble. "I'm not sure if this is the right time to talk about this, Preston," he says.

"There's never going to be a right time," I answer.

We both know that it's true. And of all the wrong times to talk, maybe this time is the best we'll ever get.

I sit down across from him, and Dad closes his eyes, as if to pray for the right words to come.

24

WHAT DAD DID

"I loved your mother, Preston," Dad says as we sit in the middle of the ruined living room. "I know it sounds funny, but I did. I think she wanted to leave me for a long time—but she wouldn't leave you kids, and I don't think she had the heart to leave me while I still loved her. So I think she tried her best to just make me stop loving her."

I watch his eyes as he speaks. I watch his every gesture, looking for lies or cover-ups—but everything he says has such a ring of truth, I have to believe him.

He tells me how they were each other's first love—a fact I knew, but it never occurred to me that Dad met Mom when he was younger than I am now. They were going steady at fifteen, while I can't even stick with the same girlfriend for more than a couple of months at a time. He was so young. "I remember I baked her a cake on her sixteenth birthday," he says. "God, I was just a kid.

"You see, I never felt I was good enough to keep her," says Dad. "I thought it was a miracle she went out with me, much less married me. And I treated her like a queen at first. Gave her whatever she wanted . . . but after a while she wanted so much, I didn't know what to do. She started measuring us against all our friends who were richer than we were."

I remember some of that. I always remember feeling that our house was big, but for Mom it wasn't big enough—and our cars were nice, but they just weren't as nice as they ought to be.

"And then after Tyler was born," says Dad, "your mom finally made it clear *I* wasn't good enough. After she had him, she decided she'd had enough, period."

"Enough kids?" I ask.

"No, Preston, just *enough*. She wouldn't *be* with me, Preston. We lived in the same house for five more years, but I knew she didn't want to share it with me—and the more I told her I loved her, the more she pushed me away."

I have to keep reminding myself that it's my mother he's talking about. How could my mother be cold toward anyone? All I can remember after four years are the good things about her. But yet I know that Mom couldn't have been perfect, and I know Dad can't be lying.

"Don't get me wrong, Preston," says Dad. "Your mother

was a wonderful woman, but, you see, I pushed her into a corner, and she had to push back."

"You guys should have just got divorced," I tell Dad.

Dad shakes his head. "I can say that now, but then I would rather have died. I thought divorce was for other people. I thought if I loved her enough, it would be enough for both of us, and if I waited, she would love me again, too.

"But it only got worse, Preston. I was so frustrated, I started to smother her—and I would make a big deal out of everything she did that I felt was wrong. Pretty soon she started telling people she never did love me, that she married me just to get out of the house. I don't know if she really believed that, but she said it—maybe to get back at me for how I was treating her."

Dad grits his teeth, angry at himself now. "I was such a jealous bastard," he says, and he tells me how he wouldn't let her wear bikinis, and wouldn't let her go out with her girl-friends for fear that she would meet another guy she liked better than Dad. It was as if Dad were trying to keep her locked away from everyone else.

"I would yell at her, and she would humiliate me," says Dad, "make me feel like I wasn't a man—worse, like I wasn't a human being. I don't even think she did it intentionally. She was just angry and confused, and she took it out on me. I just couldn't take it.

"And we'd fight," says Dad.

If there's anything I can remember it was those fights. They would say horrible things to each other. "I would tell her she was a terrible wife and mother," says Dad. "She would tell me that if we got divorced, she would make sure I would never see you boys again. We didn't mean any of those things, but words like that, they stick in your head and don't go away."

Dad takes a moment to catch his breath and slow his tears. I can understand and accept all he's saying, but still, it's not enough.

"That's still no reason to kill someone," I say.

"Of course it's not," says Dad. "Don't you think I know that?"

He wipes his eyes and continues. "You see . . . I think in some strange way, I started to hate myself, and hate her, too. I hated the way she made me feel. I hated the fact that she would never take anything I said seriously. I hated her almost as much as I loved her, and it drove me crazy."

I can see it all coming back to him now—the craziness, the sickness that had gotten into his head that we all saw those few weeks before Mom died.

"Do you know what it's like, Preston, to love somebody more than anything else in the world, but hate them, too?"

"Yes, I do," I whisper, frozen by the question. "I know that feeling."

"I borrowed the gun from Paul Talbert," says Dad, "right

after your mom started seeing Warren Sharp. I sort of tricked his wife into giving it to me. At the time I even thought Paul Talbert was seeing your mom. Can you believe that? I know she spoke to him the day she threw me out, and I blamed him for that."

Dad stops for a moment. I can see how hard it is for him to talk about, but he's making himself do it. He's making himself talk because I asked him. I knew he'd find the courage to tell me if I asked him.

"Anyway," says Dad, "I held the gun for a few weeks. I figured I'd show it to your mom and threaten to kill myself. I thought I might even do that, too—but mostly I just wanted her to see it so that she'd take me seriously for once. That's all I really wanted with the gun—to get her to see that I was serious. . . . But she didn't take me seriously. In fact, she said I was ridiculous. And then she turned her back to me and started signing checks like I wasn't even in the room, and I remember feeling so small and so ridiculous that there was no reason for me to even live anymore. And I looked at her, and knew that all the love in the world wouldn't make her love me. And I hated that. I didn't know who I hated more for it—her or myself. I screamed this god-awful scream . . .

"And then the next thing I knew, I woke up in the hospital. I knew I must have shot myself—I could tell from the pain in my gut. I knew because I remembered having the gun, but that's all I remembered. And I asked the nurse how your mom was . . . figuring she called the ambulance or took me to the hospital herself. I asked how she and you boys were . . ."

Dad can barely speak through his tears now. The words come out of his throat a raspy croak. "And I remember the thing that was going through my mind over and over again, before I found out that I'd killed her. . . . I kept thinking, Now she'll take me seriously. . . . Now she'll take me seriously. . . ."

Dad breaks down, giving in to the tears completely. There are no more words left in him. Nothing but sorrow. If he had a gun, I think he would finish the job right here and now and take his own life. But I won't let him.

I put my arm around him and hold him close. *It's okay, Dad. Let me be the dad for a while,* I want to tell him. *Let me comfort you. Let me be there for you.*

I feel like rubbing his head and scratching his hair like he used to do to me, but I know that it would somehow humiliate him even further. So I lean my head up against his chest.

"Rub my hair, Dad, like you used to." He looks at me but doesn't move. "Please, Dad, I want you to. I don't care if I'm fifteen—I want you to."

Gently my father begins to rub his tear-moistened hands across my scalp. After all these years, it still makes me squint my eyes like a cat being petted between the ears.

"You should have hated me, Preston," he says. "You all should have hated me."

"I know," I admit. "I sort of did."

"I can never give you back what I took away," he says.

"I know that, too," I tell him, "but it's okay." I close my eyes and give in to the calm feeling as he holds me like a father should hold his kid. I finally feel an invisible quilt wrapping around me.

"I forgive you, Dad," I whisper. "I forgive you."

And as I say it, I realize that in all these years—in all those dozens of times I've said those words—this time, sitting here in the wreckage of our home, is the first time I've ever meant it.

25

EPILOGUE: NORMAL PEOPLE

January—Five Years Later

I explode from the blocks with a perfectly controlled blast of energy. I will be relentless today. I will make this first meet of the season the best meet of my life.

Everything seems to have fallen into place for this meet, and as I take the lead, even before the first turn, I begin to think about how my life has finally fallen into place, too. The thing with Sarah seems like such a small part of our lives now. Our house was fixed, because things can be replaced, and Sarah packed up with her kids and moved to Seattle, because people go on with their lives.

So now things are normal. I go to school, we eat dinner, go to church on Sundays. Dad and I have arguments like most sixteen-year-olds and their parents. Normal.

As I round the first turn, for an instant I can swear I catch sight of my family in the stands. I know they're all there: Aunt Jackie, Grandma, Tyler, Dad. Everyone but Uncle Steve.

Uncle Steve still doesn't talk to Dad. There are probably a lot of people who'd do the same—a lot of people who would say that my grandmother's Peace after she found out my mom had died was just plain old shock—and that the healing that took place in our lives isn't healing at all—it's just denial.

People have a right to say that, I guess.

And I have a right not to listen.

The final turn. I get to thinking about this thing I saw the other night on *60 Minutes*. Same story as ours—the dad goes nuts and kills the mom. The woman's parents get custody of the kids, and then what do they do? The grandparents teach the kids to hate the father for what he did.

Then the father gets out of prison. He fights to get the kids back again, and when he does, he teaches them to hate the grandparents. Then the grandparents sue to get the kids back a second time. In the end, everybody hates everybody, the whole family's all screwed up in the head and miserable, and only their lawyers, who are getting richer than Midas, seem happy about the whole thing.

Personally I think our way is a whole lot better.

I'm in the stretch, and I'm so far in the lead, I can't see any of the other runners. I blast across the finish line, and for the first time, I know for a fact that I am fast enough!

The crowd cheers, and Grandpa, who is still my private

coach, hurries up to me with the news, but he doesn't have to tell me—I know: it's a new school record.

"Yes!" I throw back my head in triumph. Up above, the clouds hang in perfect balance between the earth and the sky. I think of Mom and wonder whether or not she's cheering for me. It's been almost five years now. It took me quite a while to realize that even if Mom did roll over in her grave, like the district attorney said, it certainly didn't stop her from loving me or Tyler, or Grandma or Grandpa.

Actually, she's probably at peace with this whole business now, because from where she sits in heaven, the troubles we go through down here probably don't seem all that important.

When the meet is over, the good feeling doesn't just slip away like it used to—it lingers in the air, and while everyone else is clearing the stands and jamming the parking lot, my family comes down as they always do. Grandma gives me her big kiss and tells me how proud she is of me, and Dad and Tyler both give me hugs.

"You'll probably break *my* records someday," I tell Tyler.

"You really think so?" he asks with his trademark smile—wider now that all of his teeth are in.

Smile or not, though, I do worry about Tyler. In lots of ways, he still doesn't quite get it. He'll seem fine, and then out of nowhere he'll come home with a picture he drew in school of Dad shooting Mom. And below it, a caption: "Bad,

Bad, Dad." Someday, when he's old enough, Tyler will have to have it out with Dad like I did, and Dad will have to explain to him about what he did to Mom. I don't think it's something Dad can hide from, and I don't think he should try. It may be his last responsibility to our mother.

I hand Tyler the record-breaking medal to hold, and he examines it, probably wondering why it doesn't look any different from the other ones.

Yes, Tyler will be okay. I have to believe that. Just like I have to believe that Mom is watching, cheering me on—and that a day will come when I will finally see her, and she'll hold me with such a powerful embrace, it will make up for all the embraces we've missed over the years. But that's a long way off. For now, I have enough love around me to last a lifetime.

Jason hangs in the background like he always does during the family emotional stuff. Finally he comes up to me and pats me on the back. "Congratulations," he says. "Today the pizza's my treat." Which is easy for him to say; he works at the pizza place, so he gets it for free.

"I'll meet you there," I tell him. Grandma and Grandpa have headed to their car with Tyler, but Dad is still here. He stands alone, looking down the track, thinking. I know he was a track star when he was in high school, but I don't know what his best events were. There are just so many things you never get to know about your parents.

"Ah, you're not so fast," says Dad with a smirk on his face.

I play along with him. "No, I'm not. Actually, I'm pretty slow, compared to a Porsche. And a Porsche doesn't even break a sweat."

"Exactly," he says, and his smirk widens. "You've never beaten me in a race, you know."

"Last time I raced you, I was eleven years old!"

"So?"

It's a challenge, and the two of us get down in starting position, at the finish line, facing the wrong way on the track.

"Okay," says my dad, "on your mark . . ." And then he takes off. I knew he'd take off before he said "go"—but I wasn't expecting him to start running before he said "get set." I stumble but get right back to my feet, laughing. At twenty yards, I catch up with him and slow down, letting him stay neck and neck with me. We never did say where the finish line was going to be, so we both just keep running.

Now, as the ash pounds beneath our feet, it suddenly doesn't seem to matter whether forgiving my father is right or wrong.

Because now I'm running *with* my dad, instead of away from him, and that's the way I like it.

AFTERWORD

In his senior year of high school, Preston Scott was offered scholarships in football and track from numerous universities.

Some time after the incident with Sarah, Danny Scott fell in love with a woman who knew his background but loved him in spite of it. After a long engagement, they were married.

Preston was Danny's best man.